The Opening and Closing Lines of Novels

This book is dedicated to my parents.

The Opening and Closing Lines of Novels

The Opening and Closing Lines of Novels has a distinctive format. The reader is presented the opening lines of a particular classic and these lines are followed by the closing lines of the same classic; both segments are separated by an ellipsis. Below the opening and closing lines are three different choices of titles with their respective authors. They are numbered 1, 2, and 3 respectively. The correct number will appear at the top of the next page where the openings and closings of another novel begin. The reader must decide which title and author corresponds to the classic in question. The other two incorrect choices are still accurate and help the reader to learn titles with their authors.

Having read all the classics in question is not a prerequisite to appreciating how these novelists made their entrances and exits from the work under scrutiny. Using ones powers of observation and deduction can lead to a good choice. Clues exist throughout the presentations. Places reveal locations while dates reveal eras. The actual writing reveals genre and style while language can disclose time periods. Finally, phrasing demonstrates the author's signature or personal touch. Aside from this, some clues that could easily give away the title or author of the work have been hidden.

If you aspire to be a writer of any sort, or wish to take a try at it, these openings and closings can be used as an example of all the various approaches that are available for someone like you. Not everyone has the end of a piece in site, but one can jot down some ideas to begin a work. By noting how these novelists use figures of speech and pronunciation to make their point, you will begin to see that you can develop any style of writing that suits you. It does not mean that you have to break every rule in the book; poetic license has its limits if we want to communicate our thoughts to the reader.

"Who is John Galt?"

The light was ebbing, and Eddie Willers could not distinguish the bum's face. The bum had said it simply, without expression. But from the sunset far at the end of the street, yellow glints caught his eyes, and the eyes looked straight at Eddie Willers, mocking and still-as if the question had been addressed to the causeless uneasiness within him.

"Why did you say that?" asked Eddie Willers his voice tense.

The bum leaned against the side of the doorway; a wedge of broken glass behind him reflected the metal yellow of the sky.

"Why does it bother you?" he asked.

"It doesn't," snapped Eddie Willers.

He reached hastily into his pocket. The bum had stopped him and asked for a dime, then had gone on talking, as if to kill that moment and postpone the problem of the next. Pleas for dimes were so frequent in the streets these days that it was not necessary to listen to explanations, and he had no desire to hear the details of this bum's particular despair.

***

They could not see the world beyond the mountains, there was only a void of darkness and rock, but the darkness was hiding the ruins of a continent: the roofless homes, the rusting tractors, the lightless streets, the abandoned rail. But far in the distance, on the edge of the earth , a small flame was waving in the wind, the defiantly stubborn flame of Wyatt's Torch, twisting, being torn and regaining its hold, not to be uprooted or extinguished. It seemed to be calling and waiting for the words John Galt was now to pronounce.

"The road is cleared," said Galt. "We are going back to the world."

He raised his hand and over the desolate earth he traced in space the sign of the dollar.

1. THE FOUNTAINHEAD by Ayn Rand
2. ATLAS SHRUGGED by Ayn Rand
3. ANTHEM by Ayn Rand

7

2

He lay flat on the brown, pine-needled floor of the forest, his chin on his folded arms, and high overhead the wind blew in the top of the pine trees. The mountainside sloped gently where he lay; but below it was steep and he could see the dark of the oiled road winding through the pass. There was a stream alongside the road and far down the pass he saw a mill beside the stream and the falling water of the dam, white in the summer sunlight.

"Is that the mill?" he asked.

"Yes."

"I do not remember it."

"It was built since you were here. The old mill is further down; much below the pass."

He spread the photostated military map out on the forest floor and looked at it carefully. The old man looked over his shoulder. He was a short and solid old man in a black peasant's smock and gray iron-stiff trousers and he wore rope-soled shoes. He was breathing heavily from the climb and his hand rested on one of the two heavy packs they had been carrying.

* * *

At that distance there would be no problem. The officer was Lieutenant Berrendo. He had come up from La Granja when they had been ordered up after the first report of the attack on the lower post. They had ridden hard and had then had to swing back, because the bridge had been blown, to cross the gorge high above and come around through the timber. Their horses were wet and blown and they had to be urged into the trot.

Lieutenant Berrendo, watching the trail, came riding up, his thin face serious and grave. His submachine gun lay across his saddle in the crook of his left arm. Robert Jordan lay behind the tree, holding onto himself very carefully and delicately to keep his hands steady. He was waiting until the officer reached the sunlit place where the first trees of the pine forest joined the green slope of the meadow. He could feel his heart beating against the pine needle floor of the forest.

1. THEMILL OF THE FLOSS by George Eliot

2. FOR WHOM THE BELLS TOLL by Ernest Hemingway

3. FAR FROM THE MADDING CROWD by Thomas Hardy

2

If you really want to hear about it, the first thing you'll probably want to know is where I was born, and what my lousy childhood was like, and how my parents were occupied and all before they had me, and all that David Copperfield kind of crap, but I don't feel like going into it, if you want to know the truth. In the first place, that stuff bores me, and in the second place, my parents would have about two hemorrhages apiece if I told anything pretty personal about them. They're quite touchy about something like that, especially my father. They're *nice* and all - I'm not saying that - but they're also touchy as hell. Besides, I'm not going to tell you my whole goddam autobiography or anything. I'll just tell you about the madman stuff that happened to me around last Christmas just before I got pretty run-down and had to come out here and take it easy. I mean that's all I told D.B. about, and he's ,my *brother* and all. He's in Hollywood. That isn't too far from this crumby place, and he comes over and visits me practically every week end. He's going to drive me home when I go home next

* * *

A lot of people, especially this one psychoanalyst guy they have here, keeps asking me if I'm ' going to apply myself when I go back to school next September. It's such a stupid question, in my opinion. I mean how do you know what you're going to do until you *do* it? The answer is, you don't. I *think* I am, but how do I know? I swear it's a stupid question.

D. B. isn't as bad as the rest of them, but he keeps asking me a lot of questions, too. He drove over last Saturday with this English babe that's in his new picture he's writing. She was pretty affected, but very good looking. Anyway, one time when she went to the ladies room way down in the other wing, D. B. asked me what I thought about all this stuff I just finished telling you about. I didn't know what to hell to say. If you want to know the truth, I don't *know* what I think about it. I'm sorry I told so many people about it. About all I know is, I sort of *miss* everybody I told about. Even old Stradlater and Ackley, for instance. I think I miss that goddam Maurice. It's funny. Don't ever tell anybody anything. If you do, you start missing everybody.

1. <u>FEAR AND LOATHING IN LAS VEGAS</u> by Hunter S. Thompson

2. <u>SLAUGHTERHOUSE Five</u> by Kurt Vonnegut, Jr.

3. <u>THE CATCHER IN THE RYE</u> by J. D. Salinger

3

The airplane plip-plopped down the runway to a halt before the big sign: WELCOME TO CYPRUS. Mark Parker looked out of the window and in the distance he could see the jagged wonder of the Peak of Five Fingers of the northern costal range. In an hour or so he would be driving through the pass to Kyrenia. He stepped into the aisle, straightened out his necktie, rolled down his sleeves, and slipped into his jacket. "Welcome to Cyprus, welcome to Cyprus . . . " It ran through his head. It was from *Otello*, he thought, but the full quotation slipped his mind.

"Anything to declare?" the customs inspector said.

"Two pounds of uncut heroin and a manual of pornographic art," Mark answered, looking about for Kitty.

All Americans are coimedians, the Inspector thought, as he passed Parker through. A government tourist host approached him. "Are you Mr. Mark Parker?"

"Guilty."

* * *

Dov and Jordana and Ari and Kitty and Sutherland and Sarah. Their hearts were bursting with sorrow. As Ari walked to the head of the table to take Barak's place, Sutherland touched his arm.

"If you would not be offended," Sutherland said, "I am the oldest male Jew present. May I tell the Seder?"

"We would be honored," Ari said.

Sutherland walked to the head of the table, to the place of the head of the family. Everyone sat down and opened the copy of the Haggadah. Sutherland nodded to Dov Landau to begin.

Dov cleared his throat and read "Why is this night different from all other nights of the year?"

"This night is different because we celebrate the most important moment in the history of our people. On this night we celebrate their going forth in triumph from slavery to freedom."

1. THE FIXER by Bernard Malamud

2. EXODUS by Leon Uris

3. Mila 18 by Leon Uris

2

Brrrrrrriiiiiiiiiiiiiiiiiiiinng!

An alarm clock clanged in the dark and silent room. A bed spring creaked. A woman's voice sang out impatiently:

"Bigger, shut that thing off!"

A surly grunt sounded above the tinny ring of metal. Naked feet swished dryly across the planks in the wooden floor and the clang ceased abruptly.

"Turn on the light, Bigger."

"Awright," came a sleepy mumble.

Light flooded the room and revealed a black boy standing in a narrow space between two iron beds, rubbing his eyes with the backs of his hands. From a bed to his right spoke the woman again:

"Buddy, get up from there! I got a big washing on my hands today and I want you-all out of here."

* * *

Max groped for his hat like a blind man; he found it and jammed it on his head. He felt for the door, keeping his face averted. He poked his arm through and signaled for the guard. When he was let out he stood for a moment, his back to the steel door. Bigger grasped the bars with both hands.

"Mr. Max . . . ."

"Yes, Bigger." He did not turn around.

"I'm all right, For real, I am."

"Good-bye, Bigger." "Good-bye, Mr. Max." Max walked down the corridor.

"Mr. Max!" Max paused, but did not look.

"Tell . . . .Tell Mister . . . . Tell Jan hello . . . ."

"All right, Bigger."

"Good-bye."

"Good-bye."

He still held on to the bars. Then he smiled a faint, wry, bitter smile. He heard the ring of steel against steel as a far door clanged shut.

1. <u>NOT WITHOUT LAUGHTER</u> by Langston Hughes

2. <u>NATIVE SON</u> by Richard Wright

3. <u>ANOTHER COUNTRY</u> by James Baldwin

2

In that place where they tore the nightshade and blackberry patches from their roots to make room for the Medallion City Golf Course, there was once a neighborhood. It stood in the hills above the valley town of Medallion and spread all the way to the river. It is called the suburbs now, but when black people lived there it was called the Bottom. One road shaded by beeches, oaks, maples and chestnuts, connected it to the valley. The beeches are gone now, and so are the pear trees where children sat and yelled down through the blossoms to passersby. Generous funds have been allotted to level the stripped and faded buildings that clutter the road from Medallion up to the golf course. They are going to raze the Time and Half Pool Hall, where feet in long tan shoes once pointed down from chair rungs. A steel ball will knock to dust Irene's Palace of Cosmetology, where women used to lean their heads back on sink trays and doze while Irene lathered Nu Nile into their hair. Men in khaki work clothes will pry loose the slats of Reba's Grill, where the owner cooked in her hat beause she couldn't remember the ingredients without it.

* * *

He hadn't sold fish in a long time now. The river had killed them all. No more silver-gray flashes, no more flat wide, unhurried look. No more slowing down of gills. No more tremor on the line.

Shadrack and Nell moved in opposite directions, each thinking separate thoughts about the past. The distance between them increased as they both remembered gone things.

Suddenly Nell stopped. Her eye twitched and burned a little.

"****?" she whispered, gazing at the tops of trees, "****?"

Leaves stirred; mud shifted; there was the smell of over-ripe green things. A soft ball of fur broke and scattered like dandelion spores in the breeze.

"All that time, all that time, I thought I was missing Jude." And the loss pressed down on her chest and came up into her throat. "We was girls together," she said as though explaining something. "O Lord, ****," she cried, "girl, girl, girlgirlgirl."

It was a fine cry -loud and long-but it had no bottom and it had no top, just circles and circles of sorrow.

1. BELOVED by Toni Morrison

2. Sula by Toni Morrison

3. THE BLUEEST EYE by Toni Morrison

2

And who was that?

There's always someone nobody remembers. In the group photograph only those who have become prominent or infamous or whose faces may be traced back through experiences lived in common occupy that space and time, flattened glossily.

Who could it have been? The dangling hands and the pair of feet neatly aligned for the camera, the half-smile of profile turned to the personage who was to become the centre of the preserved moment, the single image developed to a higher intensity; on the edge of this focus there's an appendage, might as well trim it off because, in the recognition and specific memory the photograph arouses, the peripheral figure was never present.

But if someone were to come along-wait!-and recognize the one whom nobody remembers, immediately another reading of the photograph would be developed. Something else, some other meaning would be there , the presence of what was taken on, along the way, then. Something secret, perhaps. Caught so insignificantly.

* * *

He and his sometimes strange father were close on their own terms; there was no financial burden, he was making plenty of money; so long as he himself didn't find a woman he really wanted to marry they could go on perfectly well living together in odd bachelordom. His colleagues rather admired him or his affection for the handsome ageing parent they encountered in the Holland Park house. Evidently he had been and artist of some kind. According to Ivan, he kept himself busy going round the exhibitions.

One winter night in that year a pipe burst, flooding outside Vera's annexe, and she put her leather jacket over pyjamas and went to turn off the main water control in the yard. The tap was tight with chlorine deposits and would not budge in hands that became clumsy with cold. She quietly entered the house. Vera always had access, with a second set of keys Zeph had given her; she kept an eye on the house while he was away on business trips or spent a few days with his family in Odensville. The keys were fronds stiff as her fingers. A thick trail of smashed ice crackling light, stars blinded her as she let her head dip back; under the swing of the sky she stood, feet planted, on the axis of the night world. Vera walked there, for a while. And then took up her way, breath scrolling out, a signature before her.

1. A WORLD OF STRANGERS by Nadine Gordimer

2. NONE TO ACCOMPANY ME by Nadine Gordimer

3. THE LYING DAYS by Nadine Gordimer

2

Aunt Hager Williams stood in her doorway and looked out at the sun. The western sky was a sulphurous yellow and the sun a red ball dropping slowly behind the trees and house-tops. Its setting left the rest of the heavens grey with clouds.

"Huh! A storm's comin'," said Aunt Hager aloud.

A pullet ran across the back yard and into a square -cut hole in an unpainted piano-box which served as the roosting-house. An old hen clucked her brood together and, with the tiny chicks, went into a small box beside the large one. The air was very still. Not a leaf stirred on the green apple-tree. Not a single closed flower of the morning-glories trembled on the back fence. The air was very still and yellow. Something sultry and oppressive made a small boy in the doorway stand closer to his grandmother, clutching her apron with his brown hands.

* * *

When Sandy and his mother started home, it was very late, butin a little Southern church in a side street, some old black worshipers were still holding their nightly meeting. High and fervently they were singing:

By an' by when de mawnin' comes,
Saints an' sinners all are gathered home . . . .

As the deep volume of sound rolled through the open door, Anjee and her son stopped to listen.

"Its like Stanton," Sandy said, "and the tent in the Hickory Woods."
"Sure is!" his mother exlaimed. "Them old folds are still singing-even in Chicago! . . . Funny how old folks like to sing that way, ain't it?"

"It's beautiful!" Sandy cried-for, vibrant and steady like a stream of living faith, their song filled the whole nignt:

An' we'll understand it better by an' by!

1. NOT WITHOUT LAUGHTER by Langston Hughes

2. THE FIRE NEXT TIME by James Baldwin

3. TAMBOURINES TO GLORY by Langston Hughes

1

You better not never tell nobody but God. It'd kill your memory.

Dear God,

I am fourteen years old. (I am) I have always been a good girl. Maybe you can give a sign letting me know what is happening to me.

Last spring after little Lucious come I heard them fussing. He was pulling on her arm. She say It too soon, Fonso, I ain't well. Finally, he leave her alone. A week go by, he pulling on her arm again. She say Naw, I ain't gonna. Can't you see I'm already half-dead, and all of these children.

She went to visit her sister doctor over Macon. Left me to see after the others. He never had a kine word to say to me. Just say You gonna do what your mammy wouldn't. First he put his thing up gainst my hip and sort of wiggle it around. Then he grab hold my tities. Then he push his thing inside my pussy. When that hurt, I cry. He start to choke me, saying You better shut up and git used to it.

* * *

Everybody make a lot of miration over Tashi. People look at her and Adam's scars like that;s they business. Say they n ever suspect African ladiescould look so *good.* They make a fine couple. Speak a little funny, but us gitting use to it.

What your people love best to eat over there in Africa? us ast.

She sort of blush and say *barbecue.*

Everybody laugh and stuff her with one more piece.

I feel a little peculiar round the children. For one thing, they grown. And I see they think me and Nettie and Shug and Albert and Samuel and harp and Sofia and Jack and Odessa real old and don't know much what going on. But I don't think us feel old at all. And us so happy. Matter of fact, I think this the yougest us ever felt;

Amen

1. <u>THE TEMPLE OF MY FAMILIAR</u> by Alice Walker
2. <u>THE COLOR PURPLE</u> by Alice Walker
3. <u>MERIDIAN</u> by Alice Walker

2

From the small crossed window of his room above the stable in the brickyard, Yakov Bok saw people in their long overcoats running somewhere early that morning, everybody in the same direction. Vey iz mir, he thought uneasily, something bad has happened. The Russians, coming from streets around the cemetery, werehurrying, singly or in groups, in the spring snow in the direction of the caves in the ravine, some running in the middle of the slushy cobblestone streeets. Yakov hastily hid the small tin can in which he saved silver rubles, then rushed down to the yard to find out what the excitement was about. He asked Proshko, the foreman, loitering near the smoky brickkilns, but Proshko spat and said nothing.

* * *

One thing I've learned, he thought, there's no such thing as an unpolitical man, especially a Jew. You can't be one without the other, that's clear enough. You can't sit still and see yourself destroyed.

Afterwards he thought, Where there's no fight for it there's no freedom. What is it Spinoza says? If the state acts in ways that are abhorrent to human nature it's the lesser evil to destroy it. Death to the anti-Semites! Long live revolution! Long live liberty!

The crowds lining both sides of the street were dense again, packed tight between curb and housefront. There were faces at every window and people standing on roof-tops along the way. Among those in the street were Jews from the Plossky District. Some, as the carriages clattered by and they glimpsed the *****, were openly weeping, wringing their hands. One thinly bearded man clawed his face. One or two waved at Yakov. Some shouted his name.

1. DUBIN'S LIVES by Bernard Malamud

2. THE FIXER by Bernard Malamud

3. THE ASSISTANT by Bernard Malamud

2

We slept in what had once been the gymnasium. The floor was of varnished wood, with stripes and circles painted on it, for the games that were formerly played there; the hoops for the basketball nets were still in place, though the nets were gone. A balcony ran around the room, for the spectators , and I thought I could mell, faintly, like an afterimage, the pungent scent of sweat, shot through with the sweet taint of chewing gum and perfume from the watching girls, felt-skirted as I knew from pictures , later in miniskirts, then in pants, then in one earring, spiky green-streaked hair. Dances would have been held there, the music lingered, a palimpsest of unheard sound, style upon style, and undercurrent of drums, a forlorn wail, garlands made of tissue-paper flowers, cardboard devils, a revolving ball of mirrors, powdering the dancers with a snow of light.

There was old sex in the room and loneliness, and expectation of something without a shape or name. I remember that yearning for something that was always about to happen and was never the same as the hands that were on us there and then, in the small of the back, or out back,

***

The Commander put his hand to his head. What have I been saying, and to whom, and which one of his enemies has found out? Possibly he will be a security risk, now. I am above him, looking down; he is shrinking. There have already been purges among them, there will be more. Serena Joy goes white.

"Bitch," she says. "After all he did for you."

Cora and Rita press through from the kitchen. Cora has begun to cry. I was her hope, I failed her. Now she will always be childless.

The van waits in the driveway, its double doors stand open. The two of them, one on either side now, take me by the elbows to help me in. Whether this is my end or a new beginning I have no way of knowing. I have given myself over into the hands of strangers, because it can't be helped.

And so I step up, into the darkness within, or else the light.

1. <u>CAT'S EYE</u> by Margaret Atwood

2. <u>THE BLIND ASSASSIN</u> by Margaret Atwood

3. <u>THE HANDMAIDEN'S TALE</u> by Margaret Atwood

3

I am a ********** ***. No, I am not a spook like those who haunted Edgar Allan Poe; nor am I one of your Hollywood-movie ectoplasms. I am a man of substance, of flesh and bone, fiber and liquids-and I might even be said to possess a mind. I am ********, understand, simply because people ***** ** *** **. Like the ******** ***** you see sometimes in circus sideshows, it is as though I have been surrounded by mirrors of hard, distorting glass. When they approach me they see only my surroundings, themselves, or figments of their imagination-indeed, everything and anything ****** **.

Nor is my *********** exactly a matter of a biochemical accident to my epidermis. That *********** to which I refer occurs because of a peculiar disposition of the eyes of those with whom I come in contact. A matter of the construction of their *inner* eyes, those eyes with which they look through their physical eyes upon reality. I am not complaining, nor am I protesting either. It is sometimes advantageous to be ******, although it is most often rather wearing on the nerves.

* * *

Old Bad Air us still around with his music and his dancing and his diversity, and I'll be up and around with mine. And, as I said before, a decision has been made. I'm shaking off the old skin and I'll leave it here in the hole. I'm coming out, no less ******** without it, but coming out nevertheless. And I suppose it's damn well time. Even hibernations can be overdone, come to think of it. Perhaps that's my greatest social crime, I've overstayed my hibernation, since there's a possibility that even an ******** *** has a socially responsible role to play.

"Ah," I can hear you say, "so it was all a build-up to bore us with his buggy jiving. He only wanted us to listen to him rave!" But only partially true: Being ******** and without substance, a ************ voice, as it were, what else could I do? What else but try to tell you what was really happening when your eyes were ******* ********? And it is this which frightens me.

Who knows but that, on the lower frequencies, I speak for you?

1. THE QUEST OF THE SILVER FLEECE by W. E. B. Dubois

2. JUNETEENTH by Ralph Ellison

3. THE INVISIBLE MAN by Ralph Ellison

3

Boys are playing basketball around a telephone pole with a backboard bolted to it. Legs, shouts. The scrape and snap of Keds on loose alley pebbles seems to catapult their voices high into the moist March air blue above the wires. ******* Angstrom, coming up the alley in a business suit, stops and watches, though he's twenty-six and six three. So tall, he seems an unlikely *******, but the breadth of white face, the pallor of his blue irises, and a nervous flutter under his brief nose as he stabs a cigarette into his mouth partially explain the nickname, which was given to him when he too was a boy. He stands there thinking, the kids keep coming, they keep crowding you up.

His standing there makes the real boys feel strange. Eyeballs slide. They're doing this for themselves, not as a show for some adult walking around town in a double-breasted cocoa suit. It seems funny to them, an adult walking up the alley at all. Where's his car? The cigarette makes it more sinister still.

* * *

Its smallness fills him like a vastness. It's like when they heard you were great and put two men on you and no matter which way you turned you bumped into one of them and the only thing to do was pass. So you passed and the ball belonged to the others and your hands were empty and the men on you looked foolish because in effect there was nobody there.

***** comes to the curb but instead of going to his right and around the block he steps down, with as big a feeling as if this little side-street is a wide river, and crosses. He wants to travel to the next patch of snow. Although this block of three-stories is just like the one he left, something in it makes him happy; the steps and window sills seem to twitch and shift in the corner of his eye, alive. This illusion trips him. His hands lift of their own and he feels the wind on his ears even before, his heels hitting heavily on the pavement at first but with an effortless gathering out of a kind of sweet panic growing lighter and quicker and quieter, he runs. Ah: runs. Runs.

1. HERZOG by Saul Bellow

2. RABBIT RUN by John Updike

3. NOVEL TITLE by Philip Roth

2

A green hunting cap squeezed the top of the fleshy balloon of a head.. The green ear flaps, full of large ears and uncut hair and the fine bristles that grew in the ears themselves, stuck out on either side like turn signals indicating two directions at once. Full, pursed lips protruded beneath the bushy black moustache and, at their corners, sank into little folds filled with disapproval and potato chip crumbs. In the shadow under the green visor of the cap Ignatius j. Reilly's supercilious blue and yellow eyes looked down upon the other people waiting under the clock at the D. H. Holmes department store, studying the crowd of people for signs of bad taste in dress. Several of the outfits, Ignatius noted, were new enough and expensive enough to be properly considered offensive against taste and decency. Possession of anything new or expensive only reflected a person's lack of theology and geometry; it could even cast doubts upon one's soul.

* * *

Now that Fortuna had saved him from one cycle, where would she spin him now? The new cycle would be so different from anythins he had ever known.

Myrna prodded and shifted the Renault through the city traffic masterfully, weaving in and out of impossibly narrow lanes until they were clear of the last twinkling streetlight of the last swampy suburb. Then they went in darkness in the center of the salt marches. Ignatius looked out at the highway marker that reflected their headlights. US 11. The marker flew past. He rolls down the window an inch or two and breathes the salt air blowing in over the marshes from the Gulf.

As if the air were a purgative, his valve opened. He breathes again, this time more deeply. A dull headache was lifting.

He stared gratefully at the back of Myrna's head, at the pigtail that swung innocently at his knee. Gratefully. How ironic, I thought. Taking the pigtail in one of his paws, he pressed it warmly to his wet moustache.

1. NOVEL TITLE by Novel Author

2. THE CONFEDERACY OF DUNCES by John Kennedy Toole

3. NOVEL TITLE by Novel Author

I am going to pack my two shirts with my other socks and my best suit in the little blue cloth my mother used to tie round her hair when she did the house, and I am going from the *****.

This cloth is much too good to pack things in and I would keep it in my pocket only there is nothing else in the house that will serve, and the lace straw basket is over at Mr. Tom Harries', over the mountain. If I went down to Tossall the Shop for a cardboard box I would have to tell him why I wanted it, then everybody would know I was going. That is not what I want, so it is the old blue cloth, and I have promised it a good wash and iron when I have settled down, wherever that is going to be...

* * *

If Mr. Guffydd dead, him, that one of rock and flame, who was friend and mentor, who gave me his watch that was all in the world he had, because he loved me? Is he dead, and the tears still wet on my face and my voice cutting through rocks in my throats for minutes while I tried to say good-bye, and O God, the words were shy to come, and I went from him wordless, in tears and with blood.

Is he dead?

For if he is, then I am dead, and we are dead, and all of sense a mockery. ****************, then, and the **** of them that have gone.

1. HOW GREEN WAS MY VALLEY by Richard Llewellyn

2. GREEN MANSIONS by W.H. Hudson

3. BABBITT by Sinclair Lewis

1

I came to Warley on a wet September morning with the sky the GREY of Guiseley sandstone. I was alone in compartment. I remember saying to myself: "No more zombies, Joe, no more Zombies."

My stomach was rumbling with hunger and the drinks of the night before had left a buzzing in my head and carbonated-water sensation in my nostrils. On that particular morning even these discomforts added to my pleasure. I was a dissipated traveller–dissipated in a gentlemanly sort of way, looking forward to the hot bath, the hair-of-the-dog, the black coffee and the snooze in the silk dressing-gown.

My clothe were my Sunday best: a light grey suit...

* * *

.... minutes.

I went on crying, as if the tears would blur the image of Alice crawling round Corby Road on her two hands and knees, as if they would drown her first shrill screams and her last deliterious moans. "Oh God," I said, I did kill her. I wasn't there, but I killed her."

Eva drew my head on to her breast. "Poor darling, you mustn't take on so. You don't see it now, but it was all for the best. She'd have ruined your whole life. Nobody blames you, love. Nobody blames you."

I pulled myself away from her abruptly. "Oh my God," I said, "that's the trouble."

1. <u>THE LONELINESS OF THE LONG DISTANCE RUNNER</u> by Alan Sillitoe
2. <u>ROOM AT THE TOP</u> by John Braine
3. <u>THE LOST WEEKEND</u> by Charles Jackson

2

Alexey ******** was the third son Fyodor *********, a landowner well known in our district in his own day, and still remembered among us because of his gloomy and tragic death, which happened thirteen years ago, and which I shall describe in its proper place. For the present I will only say that this "landowner"–for so we used to call him, although he hardly spent a day of his life on his own estate–was a strange person, yet one fairly frequently to be met with, a despicable, vicious man and at the same time senseless. But he was one of those senseless people who are very capable of looking after their own affairs, and, apparently, after nothing else. Fyodor *********, for instance, began with next to nothing; his estate...

* * *

...and shall tell each other with joy and gladness all that has happened!" Alyosha answered, half laughing, half enthusiastic.

"Oh, how wonderful it will be!" cried Kolya

"Well, now we will finish talking and go to his funeral dinner. Don't be disturbed at our eating pancakes–it's a very old custom and there's something nice in that!" laughed Alyosha. "Well, let us go! And now we go hand in hand."

"And always so, all our lives hand in hand! Hurrah for *****!" Kolya cried once more. And once more the boys took up cry.

"Hurrah for ********!"

1. DEAD SOULS by Nikolai V. Gogol
2. THE BROTHERS KARAMAZOV by Fyodor Dostoevski
3. FATHERS AND SONS by Ivan Turgenev

2

Under certain circumstances there are few hours in life more agreeable than the hour dedicated to the ceremony known as afternoon tea. There are circumstances in which, whether you partake of the tea or not–some people of course never do–that situation is in itself delightful. Those that I have in mind in beginning to unfold this simple history offered an admirable setting to an innocent pastime. The implements of the little feast had been disposed upon the lawn of an old English country-house, in what I should call the perfect middle of a splendid summer afternoon. Part of the afternoon had waned, but much of it was left, and what was left was of the finest and rarest quality. Real dusk would not arrive for many hours; but...

* * *

...was not looking at her; his eyes were fastened on the doorstep. "Oh, she started–?" he stammered. And without finishing his phrase or looking up he stiffly averted himself. But he couldn't otherwise move.

Henrietta had come out, closing the door behind her, and now she put out her hand and grasped his arm. "Look here, Mr. Goodwood," she said; "just you wait!"

On which he looked up at her–but only to guess, from her face, with a revulsion, that she simply meant he was yound. She stood shining at him whith that cheap comfort, and it added, on the spot, thirty years to his life. She walked him away with her, however, as if she had given he now the key to patience.

1. PRIDE AND PREJUDICE by Jane Austin
2. VANITY FAIR by William Makepeace Thackeray
3. THE PORTRAIT OF A LADY by Henry James

3

It was the hour of twilight on a soft spring day toward the end of April in the year of Our Lord 1929, and George Webber leaned his elbows on the sill of his back window and looked out at what he could see of New York, He eye took in the towering mass of the new hospital at the end of the block, its upper floors set back in terraces, the soaring walls salmon colored in the evening light. This side of the hospital, and directly opposite, was the lower structure of the annex, where the nurses and the waitresses lived. In the rest of the block half a dozen old brick houses, squeezed together in a solid row, leaned wearily against each other and showed their backside to him.

The air was strangely quiet. All the noises...

* * *

...together. My tale is finished–and so farewell.

But before I go, I have just one more thing to tell you: Something has spoken to me in the night, and told me I shall die, I know not where. Saying:

"To lose the earth you know, for greater knowing; to lose the life you have, for greater life; to leave the friends you loved, for greater loving; to find a land more kind than home, more large than earth–

"–Whereon the pillars of this earth are founded, toward which the conscience of the world is tending–a wind is rising, and the rivers flow."

1. YOU CAN'T GO HOME AGAIN by Thomas Wolfe
2. OF MICE AND MEN by John Steinbeck
3. A FAREWELL TO ARMS by Ernest Hemingway

1

The family of Eastwood had been long settled in Sussex. Their estate was large, and their residence was at Norland Park, in the centre of their property, where, for many generations, they had lived in so respectable a manner as to engage the general good opinion if their surrounding acquaintance. The late owner of this estate was a single man who lived to a very advanced age, and who for many years of his life had a constant companion and housekeeper in his sister. But her death, which happened ten years before his own, produced a great alteration in his home; for to supply her loss, he invited and received into his house the family of his nephew Mr. Henry Dashwood, the legal inheritor of the Norland estate, and the person to whom he intended to bequeath...

* * *

...comparison with Mrs. Brandon.
Mrs. Dashwood was prudent enough to remain at the cottage without attempting a removal to Delaford; and fortunately for Sir John and Mrs. Jennings, when Marianne was taken from them, Margaret had reached an age highly suitable for dancing and not very ineligible for being supposed to have a lover.

Between Barton and Delaford there was that constant communication which strong family affection would naturally dictate; and among the merits and the happiness of Elinor and Marianne, let it not be ranked as the least considerable , that though sisters, and living almost within sight of each other, they could live without disagreement between themselves or producing coolness between their husbands.

1. JANE EYRE by Charlotte Bronte
2. BARCHESTER TOWERS by Anthony Trollope
3. SENSE AND SENSIBILITY by Jane Austen

3

During a portion of the first half of the present century, and more particularly during the latter part of it, there flourished and practiced in the city of New York a physician who enjoyed perhaps an exceptional share of the consideration which in the United States, has always been bestowed upon distinguished members of the medical profession. This profession in America has constantly been held in honor, and more successfully than elsewhere has put forward a claim to the epithet of "liberal." In a country in which, to play a social part, you must either earn your income or make believe that you earn it, the healing art has appeared an a high degree to combine two recognized sources of credit. It be- longs to the realm of the practical, which in the United States is a great recommendation;...

* * *

...care a button for me--with her confounded little dry manner."

"Was it very dry?" pursued Mrs. Penniman, with solicitude. Morris took no notice of her question; he stood musing an instant, with his hat on. "But why the deuce, then, would she ever marry?"

"Yes--why indeed?" sighed Mrs. Penniman. And then, as if from a sense of the inadequacy of this explanation, "But you will not despair--you will come back?"

"Come back? Damnation!" And Morris Townsend strode out of the house, leaving Mrs. Penniman staring. Catherine, meanwhile, in the parlor, picking up her morsel of fancywork, had seated herself with it again--for life, as it were.

1. ARROWSMITH by Sinclair Lewis
2. WASHINGTON SQUARE by Henry James
3. THE HOUSE OF THE SEVEN GABLES by Nathaniel Hawthorne

Whether I shall turn out to be the hero of my own life, or whether that station will be held by anybody else, these pages must show. To begin my life with the beginning of my life, I record that I was born (as I have been informed and believe) on a Friday, at twelve o'clock at night. It was remarked that the clock began to strike, and I began to cry, simultaneously.

In consideration of the day and hour of my birth, it was declared by the nurse, and by some sage women in the neighbourhood who had taken a lively interest in me several months before there was any possibility of our becoming personally acquainted, first, that I was destined to be unlucky in life, and secondly, that I was privileged to see ghosts and spirits: both these gifts...

* * *

... is certainly not glittering with Britannia metal. And now, as I close my task, subduing my desire to linger yet, these faces fade away. But, one face, shining on me like a Heavenly light by which I see all other objects, is above them and beyond them all. And that remains.

I turn my head, and see it, in its beautiful serenity, beside me. My lamp burns low, and I have written far into the night, but the dear presence, without which I were nothing, bears me company.

Oh Agnes, Oh my soul, so may thy face be by me when I close my life indeed; so may I, when realities are melting from me like the shadows which I now dismiss, still find thee near me, pointing upward!

1. KIDNAPPED by Robert Louis Stevenson

2. REMEMBRANCE OF THINGS PAST by Marcel Proust

3. DAVID COPPERFIELD by Charles Dickens

3

There once lived in a sequestered part of the county of Devonshire one Mr. Godfrey ********, a worthy gentleman, who taking it into his head rather late in life that he must get married, and not being young enough or rich enough to aspire to the hand of a lady of fortune, had wedded an old flame out of mere attachment, who in her turn had taken him for the same reason: thus two people who cannot afford to play cards for money, sometimes sit down to a quiet game for love.

Some ill-conditioned persons, who sneer at the life-matrimonial, may perhaps suggest in this place that the good couple would be better likened to two principals in a sparring match, who, when fortune is low and backers scarce, will chivalrously set to, for the mere pleasure of the buffeting; and in one respect indeed this comparison would hold good,...

* * *

...obliged both families to reside there, and always preserving a great appearance of dignity, and relating her experiences (especially on points connected with the management and bringing-up of children) with much solemnity and importance. It was a very long time before she could be induced to receive Mrs. Linkinwater into favour, and it is even doubtful whether she ever thoroughly forgave her.

There was one grey-haired, quiet, harmless gentleman, who, winter and summer, lived in a little cottage hard by ******* house, and when he was not there, assumed the superintendence if affairs. His chief pleasure and delight was in the children, with whom he was a child himself, and master of the revels. The little people could do nothing without dear Newman Noggs.

The grass was green above the dead boy's grave, and trodden by...

1. NICHOLAS NICKLEBY by Charles Dickens

2. DAVID COPPERFILED by Charles Dickens

3. GREAT EXPECTATIONS by Charles Dickens

1

Among other public buildings in a certain town, which for many reasons it will be prudent to refrain from mentioning, and to which I will assign no fictitious name, there is one anciently common to most towns, great or small: to wit, a workhouse; and in this workhouse was born--on a day and date which I need not trouble myself to repeat, inasmuch as it can be of no possible consequence to the reader, in this stage of the business at all events--the item of mortality whose name is prefixed to the head of this chapter.

For a long time after it was ushered into this world of sorrow and trouble, by the parish surgeon, it remained a ' matter of considerable doubt whether the child would survive to bear any name...

* * *

...humanity of heart, and gratitude to that Being whose code is Mercy and whose great attribute is Benevolence to all things that breathe, happiness can never be attained. Within the altar of the old village church there stands, a white marble tablet which bears as yet but one word: "AGNES." There is no coffin in that tomb; and may it be many, many years before another name is placed above it! But, if the spirits of the Dead ever come back to earth to visit spots hallowed by the love--the love beyond the grave--of those whom they knew in life, I believe that the shade of Agnes sometimes hovers round that solemn nook. I believe it none the less because that nook is in a Church, and she was weak and erring.

1. MOLL FLANDERS by Daniel Defoe
2. TOM JONES by Henry Fielding
3. OLIVER TWIST by Charles Dickens

3

Sitting beside the road, watching the wagon mount the hill toward her, Lena thinks, 'I have come from Alabama: a fur piece. All the way from Alabama a-walking. A fur piece.' Thinking although I have not been quite a month on the road I am already in Mississippi, further from home than I have ever been before. I am now further from Doane's Mill than I have been since I was twelve years old.

She had never even been to Doane's Mill until after her father and mother died, though six or eight times a year she went to town on Saturday, in the wagon, in a mail-order dress and her bare feet flat in the wagon bed...

* * *

...fences passing like it was a circus parade. Because after a while I says, 'Here comes Saulsbury,' and she says

"'What?' and I says,

"'Saulsbury, Tennessee,' and I looked back and saw her face. And it was like it was already fixed and waiting to be surprised, and that she knew that when the surprise come, she was going to enjoy it. And it did come and it did suit her. Because she said,

"'My, my. A body does get around. Here we aint been coming from Alabama but two months, and now it's already Tennessee.'"

1. THE RED BADGE OF COURAGE by Stephen Crane
2. HOW GREEN WAS MY VALLEY by Richard Llewellyn
3. LIGHT IN AUGUST by William Faulkner

3

My true name is so well known in the records or registers at Newgate, and in the Old Bailey, and there are some things of such consequence still depending there, relating to my particular conduct, that it is not to be expected I should set my name or the account of my family to this work. Perhaps after my death, it may be better known; at present it would not be proper, no, not tho' a general pardon should be issued, even without exceptions of persons or crimes.

It is enough to tell you, that as some of my worst comrades, who are out of the way of doing me harm, having gone out of the world by the steps and the string as I often expected to go, knew me by the name of...

* * *

...easy and we liv'd together with the greatest kindness and comfort imaginable; we are now grown old, I am come back to England, being almost seventy years of age. my ***** sixty eight, having perform'd much more than the limitted terms of my transportation. And now, notwithstanding all the fatigues and all the miseries we have both gone thro' we are both in good heart and health. My ***** remain'd there some time after me to settle our affairs, and at first I had intended to go back to ***, but at *** desire I alter'd that resolution and is come over to England also, where we resolve to spend the remainder of our years an sincere penitence for the wicked lives we have lived.

1. DAVID COPPERFIELD by Charles Dickens
2. MOLL FLANDERS by Daniel Defoe
3. KIDNAPPED by Robert Louis Stevenson

2

"Christmas won't be Christmas without any presents," grumbled ***, lying on the rug.

"It's so dreadful to be poor!" sighed *** looking down at her old dress.

"I don't think it's fair for some girls to have plenty of pretty things, and other girls nothing at all," added little ***, with an injured sniff.

"We've got father and mother and each other'" said *** contentedly, from her corner.

The four young faces on which the firelight shone brightened at the cheerful words, but darkened again as *** said sadly:...

* * *

...with the loving impetuosity which she never could outgrow. "I hope there will be more wheat and fewer tares every year," said ... softly.

"A large sheaf, but I know there's room in your heart for it. Marmee dear," added ***** tender voice.

Touched to the heart, Mrs. ***** could only stretch out her arms, as if to gather children and grandchildren to herself, and say, with face and voice full of motherly love, gratitude, and humility: "Oh, my girls, however long you may live, I never can wish you a greater happiness than this!"

1. GREAT EXPECTATIONS by Charles Dickens

2. LITTLE WOMEN by Louisa May Alcott

3. THE RED BADGE OF COURAGE by Stephen Courage

2

In my younger and more vulnerable years my father gave me some advice that I've been turning over in my mind ever since.

"Whenever you feel like criticizing any one," he told me," just remember that all the people in this world haven't had the advantages that you've had."

He didn't say any more, but we've always been unusually communicative in a reserved way, and I understood that he meant a great deal more than that. In consequence, I'm inclined to reserve all judgments, a habit that has opened up many curious natures to me and also made me the victim of not a few veteran bores. The abnormal mind is quick to detect and attach itself to this quality when it appears...

* * *

...green light at the end of Daisy's dock. He had come a long way to this blue lawn, and his dream must have seemed so close that he could hardly fall to grasp it. He did not know that it was already behind him, somewhere back in that vast obscurity beyond the city, where the dark fiends of the republic rolled on under the night.

***** believed in the green light. the orgiastic future that year by year recedes before us. It eluded us then, but that's no matter--tomorrow we will run faster, stretch out our arms farther. . . . And one fine morning-

So we beat on, boats against the current, borne back ceaselessly into the past.

1. A PORTRAIT OF THE ARTISTS AS A YOUNG MAN by James Joyce

2. THE GREAT GATSBY by F. Scott Fitzgerald

3. GREAT EXPECTATIONS by Charles Dickens

2

I was born in the year 1632, in the city of York of a good family, though not of that country, my father being a foreigner of Bremen who settled first at Hull. He got a good estate by merchandise and, leaving off his trade, lived afterward at York, from whence he had married my mother, whose relations were named *******, a very good family in that country. and from whom I was called ***** Kreutznaer; but by the usual corruption of words in England we are now called, nay, we call ourselves, and write our name "*****," and so my companions always called me.

I had two elder brothers, one of which was lieutenant- colonel to an English regiment of foot in Flanders, formerly commanded by the famous Colonel Lockhart, and was killed at the battle near Dunkirk against the Spaniards;

* * *

...I sent them also from the Brazils five cows, three of them being big with calf, some sheep, and some hogs, which, when I came again, were considerably increased.

But all these things, with an account how 300 Caribbees came and invaded them, and ruined their plantations, and how they fought with that whole number twice, and were at first defeated, and three of them killed; but at last, a storm destroying their enemies' canoes, they famished or destroyed almost all the rest and renewed and recovered the possession of their plantation and still lived upon the island.

All these things, with some very surprising incidents in some new adventures of my own, for ten years more, I may perhaps give a farther account of hereafter.

1. <u>ROBINSON CRUSOE</u> by Daniel Defoe

2. <u>TOM JONES</u> by Henry Fielding

3. <u>TRISTRAM SHANDY</u> by Laurence Sterne

1

On the pleasant shore of the French Riviera, about half way between Marseilles and the Italian border, stands a large, proud, rose-colored hotel. Deferential palms cool its flushed facade, and before it stretches a short dazzling beach. Lately it has become a summer resort of notable and fashionable people; a decade ago it was almost deserted after its English clientele went north in April. Now, many bungalows cluster near it, but when this story begins only the cupolas of a dozen old villas rotted like water lilies among the massed pines between Gausse's Hotel des Etrangers and Cannes five miles away.

The hotel and its bright tan prayer rug of a beach were one. In the early morning the distant image of Clones, the pink and cream of old fortifications...

* * *

***** that he didn't ask for the children to be sent to America and didn't answer when Nicole wrote asking him if he needed money. In the last letter she had from him he told her that he was practising in Geneva, New York, and she got the impression that he had settled down with someone to keep Louse for him. She looked up Geneva in an atlas and found it was in the heart of the Finger Lakes Section and considered a pleasant place. Perhaps, so she liked to think, his career was biding its time, again like Grant's in Galena; his latest note was post-marked from Hornell, New York, which is some distance from Geneva and a very small town; in any case he is almost certainly in that section of the country, in one town or another.

1. THE CHARTERHOUSE OF PARMA by Stendhal

2. THE AMERICAN by Henry James

3. TENDER IS THE NIGHT by F. Scott Fitzgerald

3

It was a feature peculiar to the colonial wars of North America, that the toils and dangers of the wilderness were to be encountered before the adverse hosts could meet. A wide and apparently an impervious boundary of forests severed the possessions of the hostile provinces of France and England. The hardy colonist, and the trained European who fought at his side, frequently expended months in struggling against the rapids of the streams, or in effecting the rugged passes of the mountains in quest of an opportunity to exhibit their courage in a more martial conflict. But, emulating the patience and self-denial of the practiced native warriors, they learned to overcome every difficulty; and it would seem that, in time, there was no recess of the woods...

* * *

...watering the grave of Uncas like drops of falling rain. In the midst of the awful stillness with which such a burst of feeling, coming, as it did, from the two most renowned warriors of that region, was received, Tamenund lifted his voice to disperse the multitude.

"It is enough" he said. "Go, children of the Lenape, the anger of the Manitto is not done. Why should Tamenund stay? The palefaces are masters of the earth and the taboo of the Red Men has not yet come again. My day has been too long. In the morning I saw the sons of Unamis happy and strong; and yet, before the night has come, have I lived to see the last warrior of the wise race of the *******."

1. DRUMS ALONG THE MOHAWK by Walter D. Edmonds
2. ETHAN FROME by Edith Wharton
3. THE LAST OF THE MOHICANS by James Fenimore Cooper

3

1801--I have Just returned from a visit to my landlord-- the solitary neighbour that I shall be troubled with. This is certainly a beautiful country! In all England, I do not believe that I could have fixed on a situation so completely removed from the stir of society. A perfect misanthropist's Heaven: and Mr. ******* and I are such a suitable pair to divide the desolation between us. A capital fellow! He little imagined how my heart warmed towards him when I beheld his black eyes withdraw so suspiciously under their brows, as I rode up, and when his fingers sheltered themselves, with a jealous resolution, still further in his waistcoat, as I announced my name.

'Mr. *******?' I said.

A nod was the...

* * *

...the kirk. When beneath its walls, I perceived decay had made progress, even in seven months: many a window showed black gaps deprived of glass; and slates jutted off, here and there, beyond the right line of the roof, to be gradually worked off in coming autumn storms.

I sought, and soon discovered the three headstones on the slope next the moor: the middle one gray: and half buried in heath; Edgar Linton's only harmonized by the turf, and moss creeping up its foot; *******'s still bare.

I lingered round them, under that benign sky: watched the moths fluttering among the heath and hare-bells; listened to the soft wind breathing through the grass; and wondered how any one could ever imagine unquiet slumbers for the sleepers in that quiet earth.

1. JANE EYRE by Charlotte Bronte

2. PRIDE AND PREJUDICE by Jane Austen

3. WUTHERING HEIGHTS by Emile Bronte

3

Mr Utterson the lawyer was a man of a rugged countenance, that was never lighted by a smile; cold scanty and embarrassed in discourse; backward in sentiment; lean, long, dusty, dreary, and yet somehow lovable. At friendly meetings, and when the wine was to his taste, something eminently human beaconed from his eye; something indeed which never found its way into his talk, but which spoke not only in these silent symbols of the after-dinner face, but more often and loudly in the ants of his life. He was austere with himself; drank gin when he was alone, to mortify a taste for vintages; and though he enjoyed the theatre, had not crossed the doors of one for twenty years. But he had an approved tolerance for others; sometimes wondering, almost with envy, at the high pressure of spirits involved in their misdeeds; and in any extremity...

* * *

...And indeed the doom that is closing on us both has already changed and crushed him.Half an hour from now, when I shall again and for ever reindue that hated personality, I know how I shall sit shuddering and weeping in my chair, or continue, with the most strained and fearstruck ecstasy of listening, to pace up and down this room (my last earthly refuge) and give ear to every sound of menace.

Will ***** die upon the scaffold? or will he find the courage to release himself at the last moment? God knows; I am careless; this is my true hour of death, and what is to follow concerns another than myself. Here, then, as I lay down the pen, and proceed to seal up my confession, I bring the life of that unhappy Henry to an end.

1. BILLY BUDD - FORETOPMAN by Herman Melville
2. DR. JEKYLL AND MR. HYDE by Robert Louis Stevenson
3. A TALE OF TWO CITIES by Charles Dickens

2

Buck Mulligan came from the stairhead, bearing a bowl of lather on which a mirror and a razor lay crossed. A yellow dressing gown, engirdled, was sustained gently behind him by the mild morning air. He held the bowl aloft and intoned:

-- Introibo ad altare Dei.

Halted, he peered down the dark winding stairs and called up coarsely:

--Come up, Kinch. Come up, you fearful jesuit.

Solemnly he came forward and mounted the round gunrest.

He faced about and blessed gravely thrice the tower, the surrounding country and the awaking mountains. Then, catching sight of Stephen Dedalus, he bent towards him and made rapid crosses in the air, gurgling in his throat and shaking his head. Stephen Dedalus, displeased and sleepy,...

* * *

...O that awful deepdown torrent O and the sea the sea crimson sometimes like fire and the glorious sunsets and the figtrees in the Alameda gardens yes and all the queer little streets and pink and blue and yellow houses and the rosegardens and the jessamine and geraniums and cactuses and Gibraltar as a girl where I was a Flower of the mountain yes when I put the rose in my hair like the Andalusian girls used or shall I wear a red yes and how he kissed me under the Moorish wall and I thought well as well him as another and then I asked him with my eyes to ask again yes and then he asked me would I yes to say yes my mountain flower and first I put my arms around him yes and drew him down to me so he could feel my breasts all perfume yes and his heart was going like mad and yes I said yes I will Yes.

1. THE MARBLE FAUN by Nathaniel Hawthorne

2. ULYSSES by James Joyce

3. THE RETURN OF THE NATIVE by Thomas Hardy

2

It is a truth universally acknowledged, that a single man in possession of a good fortune, must be in want of a wife.

However little known the feelings or views of such a man may be on his first entering a neighbourhood, this truth is so well fixed in the minds of the surrounding families, that he is considered as the rightful property of some one or other of their daughters.

"My dear Mr. Bennett," said his lady to him one day, "have you heard that Netherfield Park is let at last?" Mr. Bennet replied that he had not.

"But it is," returned she; "for Mrs. Long has just been here, and she told be all about it."

Mr. Bennett made no answer.

"Do not you want to know who has taken it?"...

* * *

...by Elizabeth's persuasion, he was prevailed on to overlook the offence, and seek a reconciliation; and, after a little further resistance on the part of his aunt, her resentment gave way, either to her affection for him, or her curiosity to see how his wife conducted herself; and she condescended to wait on them at Pemberly, in spite of that pollution which its goods had received, not merely from the presence of such a mistress, but the visits of her uncle and aunt from the city.

With the Gardiners, they were always on the most intimate terms. Darks, as well as Elizabeth, really loved them; and they were both ever sensible of the warmest gratitude towards the persons who, by bringing her into Derbyshire, had been the means of uniting them.

1. BARCHESTER TOWERS by Anthony Trollope
2. PRIDE AND PREJUDICE by Jane Austen
3. JANE EYRE by Charlotte Bronte

"*************," said I to myself. "I don't seem to remember hearing of it before. Name of the asylum, likely."

It was a soft, reposeful summer landscape, as lovely as a dream, and as lonesome as Sunday. The air was full of the smell of flowers, and the buzzing of insects, and the twittering of birds, and there were no people, no wagons, there was no stir of life, nothing going on. The road was mainly a winding path with hoofprints in it, and now and then a faint trace of wheels on either side of the grass—wheels that apparently had a tire as broad as one's hand.

Presently a fair slip of a girl, about ten years old, with a catract of golden hair streaming down over her shoulders, came along. Around her head she wore a hoop of flame-red poppies. It was as sweet an outfit as ever I saw, what there was of it. She walked indolently along, with a mind at rest, its...

* * *

...men! Open fire!'

The thirteen gatlings began to vomit death into the fated ten thousand. They halted, they stood their ground a moment against that deluge of fire, then they broke, faced about and swept force never reached the top of the lofty embankment; the three-fourths reached it and plunged over—to death by drowning.

Within ten short minutes after we had opened fire, armed resistance was totally annihilated, the campaign was ended, we fifty-four were masters of England! Twenty-five thousand men lay around us.

But how treacherous is fortune! In a little while—say an hour—happened a thing, by my own fault, which—but I have no heart to write that. Let the record end here.

1. THE CHATERHOUSE OF PARMA by Stendhal
2. A CONNECTICUT YANKEE IN KING ARTHUR'S COURT by Mark Twain
3. THE COUNT OF MONTE CRISTO by Alexandre Dumas, Pere

2

There was no possibility of taking a walk that day. Me had been wandering, indeed, in the leafless shrubbery an hour in the morning; but since dinner (Mrs. Reed, when there was no company, dined early) the cold winter wind had brought with it clouds so sombre, and a rain so penetrating. that further out-door exercise was now out of the question.

I was glad of it: I never liked long walks, especially on chilly afternoons: dreadful to me was the coming home in the raw twilight, with nipped fingers and toes, and a heart saddened by the chidings of Bessie, the nurse, and humbled by the consciousness of my physical inferiority to Eliza, John, and Georgiana Reed.

The said Ellza. John, and Georgiana...

* * *

...and the toil draws near its close: his glorious sun hastens to its setting. The last letter I received from him drew from my eyes human tears, and yet filled my heart with Divine joy: he anticipated his sure reward his incorruptible crown. I know that a stranger's hand will write to me next, to say that the good and faithful servant has been called at length into the joy of his Lord. And why weep for this? No fear of death will darken St. John's last hour: his mind will be unclouded; his heart will be undaunted; his hope will be sure; his faith steadfast. His own words are a pledge of this:--

"My Master," he says," has forewarned me. Daily he announces more distinctly,--'Surely I come quickly!' and hourly I more eagerly respond,-'Amen; even so come, Lord Jesus!'"

1. WUTHERING HEIGHTS by Emily Bronte
2. PRIDE AND PREJUDICE by Jane Austen
3. JANE EYRE by Charlotte Bronte

3

The map, which exaggerates the size of ******* and Blefscu (and misnames the capital of *****, properly Mildendo), locates these islands west of the Australian mainland, southeast of Sumatra, Van Diemen's Land was a name applied to both the island of Tasmania (near the southeast coast of Australia) and to the northwest mainland of Australia proper. The map confusingly gives Van Diemen's Land the shape of Tasmania (as in Herman Moll's map of the World in 1719) but places the islands as if Van Diemen's Land were the northwest mainland Arthur E. Case (Four Essays on *************, page 56) has suggested that all difficulties are resolved if we locate the isands northeast rather than northwest of Tasmania; this puts them well out to sea, where islands belong, and near the thirtieth parallel.

The map shows us two small...

* * *

...to distinguish this pride, for want of thoroughly understanding human nature as it showeth itself in other countries where that animal presides. But I, who had more experience, could plainly observe some rudiments of it among the wild *****.

But the *********, who live under the government of reason, are no more proud of the good qualities they possess than I should be for not wanting a leg or an arm, which no man in his wits would boast of, although he must be miserable without. I dwell the longer upon this subject from the desire I have to make the society of an English Yahoo by any means not insupportable, and therefore I here entreat those who have any tinctre of this absurd vice, that they will not presume to appear in my sight.

1. MOBY DICK by Herman Melville

2. TREASURE ISLAND by Robert Louis Stevenson

3. GULLIVER'S TRAVELS by Jonathan Swift

3

"***!"

No answer.

"***!"

No answer.

"What's the wrong with that boy, I wonder? You ***!"

No answer.

The old lady pulled her spectacles down and looked over them about the room; then she put them up and looked out under them. She seldom or never looked through them for so small a thing as a ***; they were her state pair, the pride of her heart, and were built for "style," not service–she could have seen through a pair of stove lids just as well. She looked perplexed for a moment, and then said, not fiercely, but still loud enough...

* * *

...reckon she'll be proud she snaked in out of the wet."

CONCLUSION

So endeth this chronicle. It being strictly a history of a ***, it must stop here; the story could not go much further without becoming the history of a ***. When one writes a novel about grown people, he knows exactly where to stop–that is, with a marriage; but when he writes of ******, he must stop where he best can.

Most of the characters that perform in this book still live, and are prosperous and happy. Some day it may seem worth while to take up the story of the younger ones again and see what sort of men and women they turned out to be; therefore it will be wisest not to reveal any of that part of their lives at present.

1. <u>TOM JONES</u> by Henry Fielding
2. <u>THE PRINCE AND THE PAUPER</u> by Mark Twain
3. <u>TOM SAWYER</u> by Mark Twain

3

The year 1797, the year of this narrative, belongs to a period which, as every thinker now feels, involved a crisis for Christendom not exceeded in its undetermined momentousness at the time by any other era whereof there is record. The opening proposition made by the Spirit of that Age involved rectification of the Old World's hereditary wrongs. In France, to some extent, this was bloodily effected. But what then? Straghtway the Revolution itself became a wrongdoer, one more oppressive than the kings. Under Napoleon it enthroned upstart kings, and initiated that prolonged agony of continual war whose final throe was Waterloo. During those years not the wisest could have foreseen that the outcome of all would be what to some thinkers apparently...

* * *

...aren't it all sham? A blur's in my eyes; it is dreaming that I am. A hatchet to my hawser? All adrift to go? The drum roll to grog, and never know? But Donald he has promised to stand by the plank; So I'll shake a friendly hand ere I sink. But–no! It is dead then I'll be, come to think.–I remember Taff the Welshman when he sank. And his cheek it was like the budding pink. But me they'll lash me in hammock, drop me deep. Fathoms down, fathoms down, how I'll dream fast asleep. I feel it stealing now. Sentry, are you there? Just ease this darbies at the wrist, and roll me over fair, I am sleepy, and the oozy weeds about me twist.

1. BILLY BUDD - FORETOPMAN by Herman Melville
2. KIDNAPPED by Robert Louis Stevenson
3. LORNA DOONE by Richard D. Blackmore

1

Mr. Jones, of the Manor Farm, had locked the hen-houses for the night, but was too drunk to remember to shut the popholes. With the ring of light from his lantern dancing from side to side, he lurched across the yard, kicked off his boots at the back door, drew himself a last glass of beer from the barrel in the scullery, and made his way up to bed, where Mrs. Jones was already snoring.

As soon as the light in the bedroom went out there was a stirring and fluttering all through farm buildings. Word had gone round during the day that old Major, the prize Middle White boar, had a strange dream on the previous night and wished to communicate it...

* * *

..uproar of voices was coming from the farmhouse. They rushed back and looked through the window again. Yes, a violent quarrel was in progress. There were shoutings, bangings on the table, sharp suspicious glances, furious denials. The source of the trouble appeared to be that Napoleon and Mr. Pilkington had each played an ace of spaces simultaneously.

Twelve voices were shouting in anger, and they were all alike. No question, now, what had happened to the faces of the pigs. The creatures outside looked from pig to man, and from man to pig, and from pig to man again; but already it was impossible to say which was which.

1. OF MICE AND MEN by John Steinbeck
2. ANIMAL FARM by George Orwell
3. ABSALOM, O ABSALOM by William Faulkner

2

All happy families are like one another; each unhappy family is unhappy in its own way.

Everything was in confusion in the Oblonsky household. The wife had found out that the husband had had an affair with their French governess and had told him that she could not go on living in the same house with him. This situation had now gone on for three days and was felt acutely by the husband and wife themselves, by all the members of the family, and by their servants. All the members of the family and the servants felt that there was no sense in their living together under the same roof and that people who happened to meet at any country inn had more in common with another than they, the members of Oblonsky family and their servants. The wife...

* * *

...know what it is–but that feeling as entered just as imperceptibly into my soul through suffering and has lodged itself there firmly.

"I shall still get angry with my coachman Ivan, I shall still argue and express my thoughts inopportunely; there will be a wall between the holy of holies of my soul and other people, even my wife, and I shall still blame her for my own fears and shall regret it; I shall still be unable to understand with my reason why I am praying, and I shall continue to pray–but my life, my whole life, independently of anything that may happen to me, every moment of it, is no longer meaningless as it was before, but has as incontestable meaning of goodness, with which I have the power to invest in it."

1. THE BROTHERS KARAMAZOV by Fyodor Dostoevski
2. FATHERS AND SONS by Ivan Turgenev
3. ANNA KARENINA by Leo Tolstoy

3

When Farmer Oak smiled, the corners of his mouth spread till they were within an unimportant distance of his ears, his eyes were reduced to chinks, and diverging wrinkles appeared round them, extending upon his countenance like the rays in a rudimentary sketch of the rising sun.

His Christian name was Gabriel, and on working days he was a young man of sound judgement, easy motions, proper dress, and general good character. On Sundays he was a man of misty views, rather given to postponing and hampered by his best clothes and umbrella: upon the whole, one who felt himself to occupy morally tat vast middle space of Laodicean neutrality which lay between the Communion people of the parish and the drunken section,–that is, he went to church, but yawned privately by...

* * *

..."It might have been a little more true to nater if't had been spoke a little chillier, but that wasn't to be expected just now.'

'That improvement will come wi' time,' said Jan, twirling his eye.

Then Oak laughed, and Bathsheba smiled (for she never laughed readily now), and their friends turned to go.

'Yes; I suppose that's the size o't,' said Joseph Poorgrass with a cheerful sigh as they moved away; 'and I wish him joy o' her; though I were once or twice upon saying today with holy Hosea, in my scripture manner, which is my second nature, "Ephraim is joined to idols: let him alone." But since 'tis as 'tis, why, it might have been worse, and feel my thanks accordingly.'

1. FAR FROM THE MADDING CROWD by Thomas Hardy

2. BARCHESTER TOWERS by Anthony Trollope

3. ABSALOM, ABSALOM! By William Faulkner

1

On the first Monday of the month of April, 1625, the borug, of Meung, in which the author of the "Romance of the Rose" was born, appeared to be in as perfect a state of revolution as if the Hugenots had just made a second Rochelle of it. Many citizens, seeing the women flying toward the High Street, leaving their children crying at the open doors, hastened to don the cuirass, and supporting their somewhat uncertain courage with a musket or a partizan, directed their steps toward the hostelry of Franc-Meunier, before which was gathered, increasing every minute, a compact group, vociferous and full of curiosity.

In those times panics were common, and few days passed without some city or other enregistering in its archives an event of this kind. There were nobles who made war against each other; there was the king, who made war...

* * *

...obtained from Rochefort the rank of sargeant in the guards.

M. Bonacieux lived on very quietly, perfectly ignorant what had become of his wife, and caring very little about the mater. One day he had the imprudence to intrude himself upon the memory of the cardinal; the cardinal had him informed that he would provide for him, so that he should never want for anything in the future. In fact, M. Bonacieux having left his house at seven o'clock in the evening to go to the Louvre, never appeared again in the Rue des Fossoyeurs; the option of those who seemed to be best informed was that he was fed and lodged in some royal castle, at the expense of his generous eminence.

1. THE THREE MUSKETEERS by Alexandre Dumas, Sr.
2. THE RED AND THE BLACK by Stendhal
3. MADAME BOVARY by Gustave Flaubert

1

It was about eleven o'clock in the morning, mid-October, with the sun not shining and a look of hard wet rain in the clearness of the foothills. I was wearing my powder-blue suit, with dark blue shirt, tie and display handkerchief, black brogues, black wool socks with dark blue clocks on them. I was neat, clean, shaved and sober, and I didn't care who knew it. I was everything the well-dressed private detective ought to be. I was calling on four million dollars.

The main hallway of the Sternwood place was two stories high. Over the entrance doors, which would have let in a troop of Indian elephants, there was a broad stained-glass panel showing a knight in dark armor rescuing a lady who was tied to a tree and didn't have any clothes on but some very long hair.

***

You just slept, not caring about the nastiness of how you died or where you fell. Me, I was a part of the nastiness now. Far more a part of it than Rusty Regan was. But the old man didn't have to be. He could lie quiet in his canopied bed, with his bloodless hands folded on the sheet, waiting. His heart was a brief, uncertain murmur. His thoughts were as gray as ashes. And in a little while he too, like Rusty Regan, would be sleeping.

On the way downtown I stopped at a bar and had a couple of double scotches. They didn't do me any good. All they did was make me think of Silver Wig, and I never saw her again.

1. THE LADY IN THE LAKE by Raymond Chandler

2. THE BIG SLEEP by Raymond Chandler

3. FAREWELL, MY LOVELY by Raymond Chandler

2

In the town they tell the story of the great *****–how it was found at how it was lost again. They tell of Kino, the fisherman, and of his wife, Juana, and of the baby Coyotito. And because the story has been told so often, it has taken root in every man's mind. And, as with all retold tales that are in people's hearts, there are only good and bad things and black and white things and good and evil things and no in-between anywhere.

"If this story is a parable, perhaps everyone takes his own meaning from it and reads his own life into it. In any case, they say the town that..."

Kino awakened in the near dark. The stars still shone and the day had drawn only a pale wash of light in the lower sky to the east. The roosters...

* * *

...splash in the distance, and they stood side by side watching the place for a long time.

And the ********* settled into the lovely green water and dropped toward the bottom. The lights on its surface were green and lovely. It settled down to the sand bottom among the fern-like plants. Above, the surface of the water was a green mirror. And the ***** lay on the floor of the sea. A crab scampering over the bottom raised a little cloud of sand, and when it settled the ***** was gone.

And the muse of the ***** drifted to a whisper and disappeared.

1. <u>LORD JIM</u> by Joseph Conrad
2. <u>THE OLD MAN AND THE SEA</u> by Ernest Hemingway
3. <u>THE PEARL</u> by John Steinbeck

3

To the red country and part of the gray country of Oklahoma, the last rains came gently, and they did not cut the scarred earth. The plows crossed and recrossed the rivulet marks. The last rains lifted the corn quickly and scattered weed colonies and grass along the sides of the roads so that the gray country and the dark red country began to disappear under a green cover. In the last part of May the sky grew pale and the clouds that had hung in the high puffs for so long in the spring were dissipated. The sun flared down on the growing corn day after day until a line of brown spread along the edge of each green bayonet. The clouds appeared, and went, and in a while they did not try any more. The weeds grew darker...

***

...boy with her; and she closed the squeaking door.

For a minute Rose of Sharon sat still in the whispering barn. The she hoisted her tired body up and drew the comforter about her. She moved slowly to the corner and stood looking down at the wasted face, into the wide, frightened eyes. Then slowly she lay down beside him. He shook his head slowly from side to side. Rose of Sharon loosened one side of the blanket bared her breast. "You got to," she said. She squirmed closer and pulled his head close. "There!" she said. "There" Her hand moved behind his head and supported it. Her fingers moved gently in his hair. She looked up and across the barn, and her lips came together and smiled mysteriously.

1. OF MICE AND MEN by John Steinbeck
2. THE GRAPES OF WRATH by John Steinbeck
3. THE RED PONY by John Steinbeck

2

The schoolmaster was leaving the village, and everybody seemed sorry. The milder at Cresscombe lent him the small white tilted cart and horse to carry his goods to the city of his destination, and twenty miles off, such a vehicle proving of quite sufficient size for the departing teacher's effects. For the school-house had been partly furnished by the managers, and the only cumbersome article possessed by the master, in addition to the packing-case of books, was a cottage piano that he had bought at an auction during the year in which he thought of learning instrumental music. But the enthusiasm having waned he had never acquired any skill in playing, and the purchased article had been a perpetual trouble to him ever since in moving house.

The rector had gone away for the...

* * *

...alive to see her, he would hardly have cared for her any more, perhaps.'

'That's what we don't know... Didn't he ever ask you to send for her, since he came to see her in that strange way?'

'No. Quite the contrary. I offered to send, and he said I as not to let her know how ill he was.'

'Did he forgive her?'

'Not as I know.'

'Well--poor little thing, 'tis to be believed she's found forgiveness somewhere! She said she had found peace!'

'She may swear that on her knees to the holy cross upon her necklace till she's hoarse, but it won't be true!' said Arabella. 'She's never found peace since she left his arms, and never will again till she's as he is now!'

1. THE RETURN OF THE NATIVE by Thomas Hardy
2. THE BRIDGE OF SAN LUIS REY by Thornton Wilder
3. JUDE THE OBSCURE by Thomas Hardy

3

We were studying when the headmaster came in, followed by a new boy, not yet wearing a school uniform, and a monitor carrying a large desk. Those of us who had been sleeping awoke, and we all stod up as if we had been interrupted in our work.

The headmaster motioned to us to sit down again; then, turning toward the teacher, he said in a low voice, "Monsieur Roger, here is a student I'm placing in your charge. He is starting in the fight. If he does well, he will advance into the upper school, where he belongs at his age."

Keeping himself in the corner behind the door so that you could hardly see him, the new arrival was a country boy, about fifteen years old and taller than any of us. His hair was cut straight across the forehead...

* * *

...of all
AND WHEREAS he committed only the fault of sometimes loosing sight of the rules that no self-respecting writer should ever break, and of forgetting that literature, like art, if it is to achieve the good work that is its mission to produce, must be chaste and pure in its form as its expression;

In these circumstances, inasmuch as it has not been sufficiently established that Pichat, ******* and Pillet have been found guilty of the offenses with which they have been charged;

The court acquits them of the accusation brought against and dismisses the charges without costs against the defendants.

1. MADAME BOVARY by Gustave Flaubert

2. GREAT EXPECTATIONS by Charles Dickens

3. THE PRINCE AND THE PAUPER by Mark Twain

1

Since Aramis' singular transformation into confessor of the order, Baisemeaux was no longer the same man. Up to that period, the place which Aramis had held in the worthy governor's estimation was that of a prelate whom he respected and a friend to whom he owed a debt of gratitude; but now he felt himself an inferior, and that Aramis was his master. He himself lighted a lantern, summoned a turnkey, and said, returning to Aramis:

"I am at your orders, monseigneur."

Aramis merelhy nodded his head, as much to say, "Very good," and signed to him with his hand to lead the way. Baisemeaux advanced, and Aramis followed him. It was a beautiful starry night; the steps of three men resounded on the flags of the terraces, and the clinking of the keys hanging from the jailer's girdle made itself heard up to the stories of the towers,...

* * *

...principal bastion; his ears, already deaf to the sounds of life, caught feebly the rolling of the drum which announced the victory. Then, clasping in his nerveless hand the baton, ornamented with its fleur-de-lis, he cast down upon it his eyes, which had no longer the power of looking upward toward heaven, all fell back, murmuring those strange words, which appeared to the soldiers cabalistic words–words which had formerly represented so many things upon earth, and which none but the dying man longer comprehended:

"***–*******, farewell till we meet again! Aramis, adieu forever!"

Of the four valiant men whose history we have related, there now no longer remained by one single body; God had resumed the souls.

1. THE MAN IN THE IRON MASK by Alexander Dumas, Sr.
2. MADAME BOVARY by Gustave Flaubert
3. THE RED AND THE BLACK by Stendhal

1

On the 15th of May, 1796, General Bonaparte made his entry into Milan at the head of that young army which had shortly before crossed the Bridge of Lodi and taught the world that after all these centuries Caesar and Alexander had a successor. The miracles of gallantry and genius of which Italy was a witness in the space of a few months aroused a slumbering people; only a week before the arrival of the French, the Milanese still regarded them as a mere rabble of brigands, accustomed invariably to flee before the troops of His Imperial and Royal Majesty; so much at least was reported to them three times weekly by a little news-sheet no bigger than one's hand, and printed on soiled paper.

In the middle Ages...

* * *

...the frontier of the States of Ernesto V. She held her court at Vignano, a quarter of a league from Casalmaggiore, on the left bank of the Po, and consequently in the Austrian states in this magnificent palace of Vignano, which the Conte had built for her, she entertained every Thursday all the high society of Parma, and every day her own many friends. Fabrizio had never missed a day in going to Vignano. The Contessa, in a word, combined all the outward appearances of happiness, but she lived for a very short time only after Fabrizio, whom she adored, and who spent but one year in his *********.

The prisons of Parma were empty, the Conte immensely rich, Ernesto V adored by his subjects, who compared his rule to that of the Grand Dukes of Tuscany.

1. THE CHARTERHOUSE OF PARMA by Stendhal
2. THE COUNT OF MONTE CRISTO by Alexander Dumas, Sr.
3. LES MISERABLES by Victor Hugo

1

Last night I dreamt I went to Manderley again. It seemed to me I stood by the iron gate leading to the drive, and for a while I could not enter, for the way was barred to me. There was a padlock and a chain upon the gate. I called in my dream to the lodge-keeper, and had no answer, and peering closer through the rusted spokes of the gate I saw that the lodge was uninhabited.

No smoke came from the chimney, and the little lattice windows gaped forlorn. Then, like all dreamers, I was possessed of a sudden with supernatural powers and passed like a spirit through the barrier before me. The drive wound away in front of me, twisting and turning as it had always done, but as I advanced I was aware that a change had come upon it; it was narrow and unkept, not the drive...

* * *

...it spread across the sky.

"It's in winter you see the northern lights, isn't it?" I said. "Not in summer."

"That's not the northern lights," he said, "that's Manderley."

I glanced at him and saw his face. I saw his eyes.

"Maxim," I said. "Maxim, what is it?"

He drove faster, much faster. We topped the hill before us and saw Lanyon lying in a hollow at our feet. There to the left of us was the silver streak of the river, widening to the estuary at Kerrith six miles away. The road to Manderley lay ahead. There was no moon. The sky above our heads was inkly black. But the sky on the horizon was not dark at all. It was shot with crimson, like a splash of blood. And the ashes blew towards with the salty wind from the sea.

1. THE RETURN OF THE NATIVE by Thomas Hardy
2. GREEN MANSIONS by W. H. Hudson
3. REBECCA by Daphne Du Maurier

3

A few miles south of Soledad, the Salinas River drops in close to the hillside bank and runs deep and green. The water is warm too, for it has slipped twinkling over the yellow sands in the sunlight before reaching the narrow pool. On one side of the river the golden foothill slopes curve up to the strong and rocky Gabilan mountains, but on the valley side the water is lined with trees–willows fresh and green with every spring, carrying in their lower leaf junctures the debris of the winter's flooding; and sycamores with mottled, white recumbent libs and branches that arch...

* * *

...looked steadily at his right hand that had held the gun.

***** twitched ****** elbow. "Come on, *****. Me an' you'll go in an' get a drink."

***** said, "You hadda, *****. I swear you hadda. Come on with me." He led George into the entrance of the trail and up towards the highway.

Curley and Carlson looked after them. And Carlson said, "Now what the hell ya suppose in eatin' them two guys?"

1. OF MICE AND MEN by John Steinbeck
2. DRUMS ALONG THE MOHAWK by Walter D. Edmonds
3. LIGHT IN AUGUST by William Faulkner

1

It was a bright cold day in April, and the clocks were striking thirteen. Winston Smith, his chin nuzzled into his breast in an effort to escape the vile wind, slipped quickly through the glass doors of Victory Mansions, though not quickly through the glass doors of Victory Mansions, thought not quickly enough to prevent a swirl of gritty dust from entering along with him.

The hallway smelt of boiled cabbage and old rag mats. At one end of it a colored poster, too large for indoor display, had been tacked to the wall. It depicted simply an enormous face, more than a meter wide: the face of a man of about forty-five, with a heavy blqack mustache and ruggedly handsome features. Winston made for the stairs. It was no use trying the lift. Even at the best of times it was seldom working, and...

* * *

...back in the Ministry of Love, with everything forgiven, his soul white as snow. He was in the public dock, confessing everything, implicating everybody. He was walking down the white-tiled corridor, with the feeling of walking in sunlight, and an armed guard at his back. The long-hoped for bullet was entering his brain.

He gazed up at the enormous face. Forty years it had taken him to learn what kind of smile was hidden beneath the dark mustache. O cruel, needless misunderstanding! O stubborn, self-willed exile from the loving breast! Two ginscented tears trickled down the sides of his nose. But it was all right, everything was all right, the struggle was finished. He had won the victory for himself. He loved ********

1. A CONNECTICUT YANKEE IN KING ARTHUR'S COURT by Mark Twain
2. OF HUMAN BONDAGE by William Somerset Maugham
3. 1984 by George Orwell

3

In the ancient city of London, on a certain autumn day in the second quarter of the sixteenth century, a boy was born to a poor family of the name of Canty, who did not want him. On the same da another English child was born to a rich family of the name of Tudor, who did want him. All England wanted him too. England had so longed for him, and hoped for him, and prayed God for him tat now that he was really come, the people went nearly mad for joy. Mere acquaintances hugged and kissed each other and cried. Everybody took a holiday, and high and low, rich and poor, feasted and danced and sang and got very mellow, and they kept this up for days and nights together. By day London was a sight to see, with gay banners waving...

* * *

...only a few years, poor boy, but he lived them worthily. More than once when some great dignitary, some gilded vassal, of the crown, made argument against his leniency and urged that some law which he was bent upon amending was gentle enough for its purpose and wrought no suffering or oppression which anyone need mightily mind, the young king turned the mournful eloquence of his great compassionate eyes upon him and answered, "What dost thou know of suffering and oppression? I and my people know, but not thou."

The reign of Edward VI was singularly merciful one for those harsh times. Now that we are taking leave of him, let us try to keep this in our minds, to his credit.

1. THE COUNT OF MONTE CRISTO by Alexander Dumas, Sr.
2. THE PRINCE AND THE PAUPER by Mark Twain
3. THE RED AND THE BLACK by Stendhal

On the human imagination events produce the effects of time. Thus, he who was traveled far and seen much is apt to fancy that has lived long, and the history that most abounds in important incidents soonest assumes the aspect of antiquity. In no other way can we account for the venerable air that is already gathering around American annals. When the mind reverts to the earliest days of colonial history, the period seems remote and obscure, the thousand changes that thicken along the links of recollections throwing back the origin of the nation to a day so distant as seemingly to reach the mists of time; yet, four lives of ordinary duration would suffice to transmit, from...

* * *

...enabled to tell our hero that Sir Robert Warley lived on his paternal estates and that there was a lady of rare beauty in the lodge who had great influence over him, though she did not bear his name. Whether this was Judith, relapsed into her early failing, or some other victim of the soldier's, ***** never knew , nor would it be pleasant or profitable to inquire. We live in a world of transgressions and selfishness, and no pictures that represent us otherwise can be true, though, happily for human nature, gleamings of that pure spirit in whose likeness man has been fashioned are to be seen, relieving its deformities and mitigating if not excusing its crimes.

1. <u>THE DEERSLAYER</u> by James Fenimore Cooper
2. <u>OF MICE AND MEN</u> by John Steinbeck
3. <u>GREEN MANSIONS</u> by W. H. Hudson

1

Squire Trelawney, Dr. Livesey, and the rest of these gentlemen have asked me to write down the whole particulars about *************, from the beginning to the end, keeping nothing back but the bearing of the island, and that only because there is still treasure not yet lifted, I take up my pen in the year of grace 17–and go back to the time when my father kept the Admiral Benbow inn the brown old seaman with the sabre cut first took up his lodging under our roof.

I remember him as if it were yesterday, as he came plodding to the inn door, his sea-chest following behind him in a hand-barrow–a tall, strong, heavy, nut-brown man, his tarry pigtail falling over the shoulders of his soiled blue coat, his hands ragged and scarred...

* * *

...formidable seafaring man with one leg has at last gone clean out of my life; but I dare say he met his old Negress, and perhaps still lives in comfort with her and Captain Flint. It is to be hoped so, I suppose, for his chances of comfort in another world are very small.

The bar silver and the arms still lie, for all that I know, where Flint buried them; and certainly they shall lie there for me. Oxen and wain-ropes would not bring me back to that accursed island; and the worst dreams that ever I have are when I hear the surf booming about its coasts r start upright in bed with the sharp voice of Captain Flint sill ringing in my ears: "Pieces of eight! Pieces of eight!"

1. SWISS FAMILY ROBINSON by Johann Rudolf Wyss
2. OMOO by Herman Melville
3. TREASURE ISLAND by Robert Louis Stevenson

3

Sir Walter Elliot, of Kellynch Hall, in Somersetshire, was a man who, for his own amusement, never took up any book but the Baronetage; there he found occupation for an idle hour, and consolation in a distressed one; thre his faculties were roused into admiration and respect, by contemplating the limited remnant of the earliest patents; there any unwelcome sensations, arising from domestic affairs, changed naturally into pity and contempt As he turned over the almost endless creations of the last century–and there, if aevery other leaf were powerless, he could read his own history with an interest which never failed–this was the page...

* * *

...might have been absolutely rich and perfectly healthy, and yet be happy. Her spring of felicity was in the glow of her spirits, as her friend Anne's was in the warmth of her heart. Anne was tenderness itself, and she had the full worth of it in Captain Wentworth's affection. His profession was all that could ever make her friends wish that tender less; the dread of a future war all that could dim her sunshine. She gloried in being a sailor's wife, but she must pay the tax of quick alarm for belonging to that profession which is, if possible, more distinguished in its domestic virtues than its national importance.

1. MOBY DICK by Herman Melville
2. MADAME BOVARY by Gustave Flaubert
3. PERSUASION by Jane Austin

3

An hour before sunset, on the evening of a day in the beginning of October, 11815 a man travelling afoot entered the little town of D******. The few persons who at this time were at their windows or their doors, regarded this traveller with a sort of distrust. It would have been hard to find a passer-by more wretched in appearance. He was a man of middle height, stout and hardy, in the strength of maturity; he might have been forty-six or seven. A slouched leather cap half hid his face, bronzed by the sun and wind, and dripping with sweat. His shaggy breast was seen through the coarse yellow shirt which at the neck was fastened by a small silver anchor; he wore a cravat twisted like a rope; coarse blue trousers, worn and shabby, white on one knee, and...

* * *

...of me a little. You are blessed creatures. I do not know what is the matter with me, I see a light. Come nearer. I die happy. Let me put my hands upon your dear beloved heads."

Cosette and Marius fell on their knees, overwhelmed, choked with tears, eadch grasping one of ********* hands. Those August hands moved no more.

He had fallen backwards, the light from the candlesticks fell upon him; his white face looked up towards heaven, he let Cosette and Marius cover his hands with kisses; he was dead.

The night was starless and very dark. Without doubt, in the gloom some mighty angel was standing, with outstretched wings, awaiting the soul.

1. THE RED AND THE BLACK by Stendhal
2. LES MISERABLES by Victor Hugo
3. MADAME BOVARY by Gustave Flaubert

2

London. Michaelmas term lately over, and the Lord Chancellor sitting in Lincoln's Inn Hall. Implacable November weather. As much mud in the streets, as if the waters had but newly retired from the face of the earth, and it would not be wonderful to meet a Megalosaurus, forty feet long or so, waddling like an elephantine lizard up Holborn Hill. Smoke lowering down from chimney-pots, making a soft black drizzle with flakes of soot in it as big as full-grown snowflakes–gone into mourning, one might imagine. For the death of Dogs, undistinguishable in mire. Horses, scarcely better, splashed to their very blinkers. Foot passengers, jostling one another's umbrellas, in a general infection of ill temper, and losing their foot-hold...

***

...they were, of course."

"My dear Dame Durden," said Allan, drawing my arm through his, "do you ever look in the glass?"

"You know I do; you see me do it."

"And don't you know that you are prettier than you ever were?"

I did not know that; I am not certain that I know it now. But I know that my dearest little pets are very pretty, and that my darling is very beautiful, and that my husband is very handsome, and that my guardian has the brightest and most benevolent face that ever was seen; and that they can very well do without much beauty in e-even supposing–

1. ALICE IN WONDERLAND by Lewis Carroll
2. THE PORTRAIT OF A LADY by Henry James
3. BLEAK HOUSE by Charles Dickens

3

The first ray of light which illumines the gloom, and converts into a dazzling brilliancy that obscurity in which the earlier history of the public career of the immortal ******* would appear to be involved, is derived from the perusal of the following entry in the Transactions of the *********** Club, which the editor of these papers feels the highest pleasure in laying before his readers, as a proof of the careful attention, indefatiguable assiduity, and nice discrimination, with which his search among the multifarious documents confided to him has been conducted.

'May 12, 1827, Joseph Smiggers, Esq., P.V.P.M.P.C., presiding. The following resolutions unanimously agreed to:- 'That this Association has heard read, with feelings...

* * *

...steadily objected to return to the scenes of their old haunts and temptations. Mr. ***** is somewhat infirm now; but he retains all his former juvenility of spirit, and may still be frequently seen, contemplating the pictures in the Dulwich Gallery, or enjoying a walk about the pleasant neighbourhood on a fine day. He is known by all the poor people about, who never fail to take their hats off, as he passes, with great respect. The children idolize him, and so indeed does the whole neighborhood. Every year, he repairs to a large family merry-making at Mr. Wardle's; on this, as on all other occasions, he is invariably attended by the faithful Sam, between whom and his master there exists a steady and reciprocal attachment which nothing but death will terminate.

1. CANDIDE by Voltaire
2. THE PICKWICK PAPERS by Charles Dickens
3. GIL BLAS by Alain Rene Le Sage

2

A Saturday afternoon in November was approaching the time of twilight, and the vast tract of unenclosed wild known as Egdon Heath embrowed itself moment by moment. Overhead the hollow stretch of whitish cloud shutting out the sky was as a tent which had the whole heath for its floor.

The heaven being spread with this pallid screen and the earth with the darkest vegetation, their meeting-line at the horizon was clearly marked. In such contrast the heath wore the appearance of an installment of night which had taken its place before its astronomical hour was come: darkness had to a great extent...

* * *

...that is very true; but you don't know all the circumstances. If it had pleased God to put an end to me it would have been a good thing for all. But I am getting used to the horror of my existence. They say that a time comes when men laugh at misery through long acquaintance with it. Surely that time comes when men laugh at misery through long acquaintance with it. Surely that time will soon come to me!"

"Your aim has always been good," said Venn. "Why should you say such desperate things?"

"No, they are not desperate. They are only hopeless; and my great regret is that for what I have done no man or law can punish me!"

1. SATURDAY NIGHT AND SUNDAY MORNING by Alan Sillitoe
2. THE VICAR OF WAKEFILED by Oliver Goldsmith
3. THE RETURN OF THE NATIVE by Thomas Hardy

3

When Caroline Meeber boarded the afternoon train for Chicago, her total outfit consisted of a small trunk, a cheap imitation alligator-skin satchel, a small lunch in a paper box, and a yellow leather snap purse, containing her ticket, a scrap of paper with her sister's address in Van Buren Street, and four dollars in money. It was in August, 1889. She was eighteen years of age, bright, timid, and full of the illusions of ignorance and youth. Whatever touch of regret at parting characterized her thoughts, it was certainly not for advantages now being given up. A gush of tears at her mother's farewell kiss, a touch in her throat when the cars...

* * *

...Oh, blind strivings of the human heart! Onward, onward, it saith, and where beauty leads, there it follows. Whether it be the tinkle of a lone sheep bell o'er some quiet landscape, or the glimmer of beauty in sylvan places, or the show of soul in some passing eye, the heart knows and makes answer, following. It is when the feet weary and hope seems vain that the heartaches and the longings arise. Know, then, that for you is neither surfeit nor content. In your rocking chair, by your window dreaming, shall you long, alone. In your rocking chair, by your window, shall you dream such happiness as you may never feel.

1.

MAIN STREET by Sinclair Lewis

2. SISTER CARRIE by Theodore Dreiser

3. HEAVEN'S MY DESTINATION by Thornton Wilder

2

The towers of Zenith aspired above the morning mist; austere towers of steel and cement and limestone, sturdy as cliffs and delicate as silver rods. They were neither citadels nor churches, but frankly and beautifully office-buildings.

The mist took pity on the fretted structures of earlier generations: the Post Office with its shingle-tortured mansard, the red brick minarets of hulking old houses, factories with stingy and sooted windows, wooden tenements colored like mud. The city was full of such grotesqueries, but the clean towers were thrusting them from the business center, and on the father hills were shining new houses, homes--they seemed--for laughter and...

* * *

...just get along. I figure out I've made about a quarter of an inch out of a possible hundred rods. Well, maybe you'll carry things on further. I don't know. But I do get a kind of sneaking pleasure out of the fact that you knew what you wanted to do and did it. Well, those folks in there will try to bully you, and tame you down. Tel 'em to go the devil! I'll back you. Take your factory job, if you want to. Don't be scared of the family. No, nor all of Zenith. Nor of yourself, the way I've been. Go ahead, old man! The world is yours!"

Arms about each other's shoulders, the ********** men marched into the living room and faced the swooping family.

1. <u>BABBITT</u> by Sinclair Lewis

2. <u>HEAVEN'S MY DESTINATION</u> by Thornton Wilder

3. <u>SISTER CARRIE</u> by Theodore Dreiser

1

At about nine o'clock in the morning at the end of November, during a thaw, the Warsaw train was approaching Petersburg; at full speed. It was so damp and foggy that it was a long time before it grew light, and even then it was difficult to distinguish out of the carriage windows anything a few yards to the right of left of the railway track. Among the passengers there were some who were returning from abroad; but it was the third-class compartments that were crowded most of all, chiefly with small business men who had boarded the train at the last stop. As usual, everyone was tired, everyone looked weary after a night's journey, everyone was chilled to the narrow, and everyone's face was pale and yellow, the colour of fog...

Two passengers had found themselves sitting.

* * *

...latest obsessions. Poor Mrs. Yepanchin was longing to be back in Russia and, according to Radomsky, she criticized everything she saw abroad bitterly and quite unfairly: 'They don't know how to bake decent bread anywhere and they freeze in their cellars like mice in winter,' she said. 'At least,' she added, pointing agitatedly to the prince, who had not shown the least sign of recognizing her- 'at least I have had a good Russian cry over this poor fellow. We've had enough of being carried away by our enthusiasms. it's high time we grew sensible. And all this, all this life abroad, and all this Europe of yours s just a delusion, and all of us abroad are a delusion. Mark my words, you'll see it for yourself!' she concluded almost angrily as she took leave of Radonsky.

1. THE IDIOT by Fyodor Dostoevski

2. FATHERS AND SONS by Ivan Turgenev

3. DEAD SOULS by Nikolai. V. Gogol

1

A throng of bearded men, in sad-colored garments and gray, steeple-crowned hats, intermixed with women, some wearing hoods, and others bareheaded, was assembled in front of a wooden edifice, the door of which was heavily timbered with oak, and studded with iron spikes.

The founders of a new colony, whatever Utopia of human virtue and happiness they might originally project, have invariably recognized it among their earliest practical necessities to allot a portion of the virgin soil as a cemetery, and another portion as the site of a prison. In accordance with this rule, it may safely be assumed that the forefathers of Boston had built the first prison-house, somewhere...

* * *

...old and sunken grave, yet with a space between, as if the dust of the two sleepers had no right to mingle. yet one tombstone served for both. All around, there were momuments carved with armorial bearings; and on this simple slap of slate--as the curious investigator may still discern, and perplex himself with the purport--there appeared the semblance of an engraved escutchon. It bore a device, a herad's wording of which might serve for a motto and brief description of our now concluded legend; so sombre is it, and relieved only by one ever-glowing point of light gloomier than the shadow:--

"ON A FIELD, SABLE, THE ******** GULES"

1. THE HOUSE OF SEVEN GABLES by Nathaniel Hawthorne

2. THE PORTRAIT OF A LADY by Henry James

3. THE SCARLET LETTER by Nathaniel Hawthorne

3

Our story opens in the mind of Luther L. (L for LeRoy) Fliegler, who is lying in his bed, not thinking of anything, but just aware of sounds conscious of his own breathing, and sensitive to his own heartbeats. Lying beside him is his wife, lying on her right side and enjoying her sleep. She has earned her sleep, for it is Christmas morning, strictly speaking, and all the day before she has worked like a dog, cleaning the turkey and baking things, and, until a few hours ago, trimming the tree. The awful proximity of his heartbeats makes Luther Fliegler begin to want his wife a little, but Irma can say no when is...

***

...and then kissed him. "I feel so sorry for Caroline. You
-I"
"Don't worry," he said. "I still get my check from the government, and I can get lots of jobs-" he cleared his throat "-in fact, that's my trouble. I was saying to Alfred P. Sloan the other day. He called me up. I meant to tell you, but It didn't seem important. So I said to Al-_"

"Who is Alfred P. Sloan?"

"My God. Here I been selling—he's president of General Motors."

"Oh. So what did you say to him?" said Irma.

1. AN AMERICAN TRAGEDY by Theodore Dreiser

2. BABBIT by Sinclair Lewis

3. APPOINTMENT IN SAMARRA by John O'Hara

3

I will begin the story of my adventures with a certain morning early in the month of June, the year of grace 1751, when I took the key for the last time out the door of my father's house. The sun began to shine upon the summit of the hills as I went down the road; and by the time I had come as far as the manse, the blackbirds were whistling in the garden lilacs, and the mist that hung around the valley in the time of the dawn was beginning to arise and die away.

Mr Campbell, the minister of Essendean, was waiting for me by the garden gate, good man! He asked me if I had breakfasted; and hearing that I lacked for nothing, he took my hand in both of his and clapped it kindly under his arm.

Said he, "I will go with you as far...

* * *

...his hand upon his fortune, the present editor inclines for the time to say farewell to David. How Alan escaped, and what was done about the murder, with a variety of other delectable particulars, may be some day set forth. That is a thing, however, that hinges on the public fancy. The editor has a great kindness for both Alan and David, and would gladly spend much of his life in their society; but in this he may find himself to stand alone. In the fear of which, and lest any one should complain of scurvy usage, he hastens to protest that all went well with both, in the limited and human sense of the word "well"; that whatever befell them, it was not dishonour, and whatever failed them, they were not found wanting to themselves.

1. KIDNAPPED by Robert Louis Stevenson

2. LORNA DOONE by Richard D. Blackmore

3. GREAT EXPECTATIONS by Charles Dickens

1

It is the Thebald, on the heights of a mountain, where a platform shaped like a crescent, is surrounded by huge stones.

The Hermit's cell occupies the background. It is built of mud and reeds, flat-roofed and doorless. Inside are seen a pitcher and a loaf of black bread; in the center, on a wooden support, a large book; on the ground, here and there, bits of rush-work, a mat or two, a basket and a knife.

Some ten paces or so from the cell...

***

...longer and longer and its frame slowly faded away. the roof of the market appeared in the distance and a cock crowed; the storm had passed; a few drops of water remained in the dust of the road and made large round spots on it. As I was very tired, I went back to bed and slept.

We felt very sad on leaving Combourg, and besides, the end of our journey was at hand. Soon this delightful trip which we had enjoyed for three months would be over. The return, like the leave-taking, produces an anticipated sadness, which gives one a proof of the insipid life we lead.

1. THE TEMPTATION OF SAINT ANTHONY by Gustave Flaubert

2. TWENTY THOUSAND LEAGUES UNDER THE SEA by Jules Verne

3. THE INVISIBLE MAN by H. G. Wells

1

While the present century was in its teens, and on one sunshiny morning in June, there drove up to the great iron gate of Miss Pinkerton's academy for young ladies, on Chiswick Mall, a large family coach, with two fat horses in blazing harness, driven by a fat coachman in a three-cornered hat and wig, at the rate of four miles an hour. A black servant, who reposed on the box beside the fat coachman, uncurled his bandy legs as soon as the equipage drew up opposite Miss Pinkerton's shining brass plate, and as he pulled the bell at least a score of young heads were seen peering out of the narrow windows of the stately old brick house...

* * *

...the arm of George (now grown a dashing young gentleman) and the Colonel seizing up his little Janey, of whom he is founder than of anything in the world—fonder even than of his History of Punjab.

"Fonder than he is of me," Emmy thinks with a sigh. But he never said a word to Amelia that was not kind and gentle, or thought of a want of hers that he did not try to gratify.

Ah! Vanitas Vanitatum! Which of us is happy in this world? Which of us has his desire? Or, having it, is satisfied?—come children, let us shut up the box and the puppets, for our play is played out.

1. SENSE AND SENSIBILTY by Jane Austin

2. VANITY FAIR by William Makepeace Thackeray

3. JANE EYRE by Charlotte Bronte

2

When you are getting on in years (but not ill, of course), you get very sleepy at times, and the hours seem to pass like lazy cattle moving across a landscape. It was like that for ***** as the autumn term progressed and days shorted till it was actually dark enough to light the gas before call-over. For *****, like some old sea captain, still measured time by the signals of the past; and well he might, for he lived at Mrs. Wickett's, just across the road from the School.

* * *

...my boys...

And soon ******* was asleep.

He seemed to peaceful that they did not disturb him to say good-night; but in the morning, as the School bell sounded for breakfast, Brookfield had the news, "Brookfield will never forget his lovableness," said Cartwright, in a speech to the school. Which was absurd, because all things are forgotten in the end. But Linford at any rate, will remember and tell the tale: I said good-bye to ******* the night before he died..."

1. RIP VAN WINKLE by Washington Irving

2. GOODBYE, MR. CHIPS by James Hilton

3. THE OLD MAN AND THE SEA by Ernest Hemingway

2

******* was beginning to get very tired of sitting by her sister on the bank, and of having nothing to do; once or twice, she had peeped into the book her sister was reading, but it had no pictures or conversation in it, "and what is the use of a book," thought ***** "without pictures or conversations?"

So she was considering in her own mind (as well as she could, for the hot day made her feel very sleepy and stupid) whether the pleasure of making a daisy chain would be worth the trouble of getting up and picking the daises, when suddenly ********* pink eyes...

* * *

...herself to how this same little sister of hers would, in the after time, be herself a grown woman; and how she would keep through all her riper years, the simple and loving heart of her childhood; and how she would gather about her other little children, and make their eyes bright and eager with many a strange tale, perhaps even with the dream of *********** of long ago; and how she would feel with all their simple sorrows, and find a pleasure in all their simple joys, remembering her own child life, and the happy summer days.

1. LITTLE DORRIT by Charles Dickens

2. ALICE IN WONDERLAND by Lewis Carroll

3. JANE EYRE by Charlotte Bronte

2

From a little after two o'clock until almost sundown of the long still hot weary dead September afternoon they say in what Miss Coldfield still called her office because her father had called it that—a dim hot airless room with the blinds all closed and fastened for forty-three summers because when she was a girl someone had believed that light and moving air carried heat and that dark was always cooler, and which (as the sun shone fuller and fuller on that side of the house) became latticed with yellow slashes full of dust motes which Quentin thought of as being flecks of the dead old dried paint itself blown inward from the scaling blinds as wind might have blown them. There was a wisteria...

* * *

...conquer the western hemisphere. Of course it won't quite be in our time and of course as they spread toward the poles they will bleach out again like the rabbits and the birds do, so they won't show up so sharp against the snow. But it will still be Jim Bond; and so in a few thousand years, I who regard you will also have sprung from the loins of African kings. Now I want you to tell me just one thing more. Why do you hate the South?"

"I don't hate it," Quentin said, quickly, at once, immediately; "I don't hate it," he said. I don't hate it he thought, painting in the cold air, the iron New England dark; I don't. I don't! I don't! I don't hate it!

1. LOOK HOMEWARD, ANGEL by Thomas Wolfe

2. ABSALOM, ABSALOM! By William Faulkner

3. TOBACCO ROAD by Erskine Caldwell

2

I confess that when first I made acquaintance with Charles Strickland I never for a moment discerned that there was in him anything out of the ordinary. Yet now few will be found to deny his greatness. I do not speak of that greatness which is achieved by the fortunate politician or the successful soldier; that is a quality which belongs to the place he occupies rather than to the man; and a change of circumstances reduces it to very discreet proportions. The Prime Minister out of office is seen, too often, to have been but a pompous rhetorician, and the General without an army is but the tame hero of a market town. The greatness of Charles Strickland was authentic. It may be that you do not like his art, but at all the events you can hardly refuse it the tribute of your interest. He disturbs and arrests. The time has passed when he was an object of ridicule, and it is no longer a mark of eccentricity.

* * *

...pair of dungarees; and at night, when the boat sailed along easily before a light breeze, and the sailors were gathered on the upper deck, while the captain and the supercargo lolled in the deckchairs, smoking their pipes, I saw him dance with another lad, dance wildly, to the wheezy music of the concertina. Above was the blue sky, and the stars, and all about the desert of the Pacific Ocean.

A quotation from the Bible came to my lips, but I held my tongue, for I know that clergymen think it a little blasphemous when the laity poach upon their preserves. My Uncle Harry, for twenty-seven years Vicar of Whitsdale, was on these locations in the habit of saying that the devil could always quote scripture to his purpose. He remembered the days when you could get thirteen Royal Natives for a shilling.

1. LORD JIM by Joseph Conrad

2. THE MOON AND SIXPENCE by William Somerset Maugham

3. GREEN MANSIONS by W. H. Hudson

2

There were fourteen officers on the Reluctant and all of them were Reserves. Captain Morton was a lieutenant-commander, and on the outside had been in the merchant marine, where he claimed to hold a master's license. Mr. LeSuer, the executive officer, also a lieutenant-commander and also ex-merchant marine, swore that the Captain held only a first mate's license. Mr. LeSuer was a capable man who kept to himself and raged against the Captain with a fine singleness of purpose. The other officers represented the miscellany of pre-war America. Ensign Keith and Ensign Moulton had been college boys...

* * *

...accounted for by the exertion. He brushed his hands together carefully and went inside on the boat deck. A little detachedly he wondered: would there be eight of them out tomorrow, or sixteen?

The Captain was sitting, reading, in the large chair of his cabin. In the cone of harsh light from the floor lamp he looked old, and not evil, but merely foolish. He glanced up at the knock on the opened door.

'Yeah,' he said gruffly, 'what is it?'

Ensign ******* leaned a casual hand on the door jamb. 'Captain,' he said easily, 'I just threw your damn ************* the side.'

1. CAPTAINS COURAGEOUS by Rudyard Kipling

2. TWO YEARS BEFORE THE MAST by Richard Henry Dana, Jr.

3. MISTER ROBERTS by Thomas Heggen

3

Verrieres is no doubt one of the prettiest small towns in Franche-Comte. Its white houses with their steep red-tiled roofs are spread out over a hillside, the slightest contours of which are marked by clumps of hardy chestnuts. The Dubs flows a few hundred feet below the town's fortifications, built long ago by the Spanish and now in ruins.

Verrieres is sheltered on the north by a high mountain chain, a spur of the Jura. The Verra's jagged peaks are covered with snow from the first cold days in October. A torrent that gushes from the mountain runs through Verriers before plunging into the Doubs and...

* * *

...The bad thing about the reign of public opinion, which, it must be added, procures <u>liberty</u>, is that it meddles with that which is none of its business; for instance, private life. Hence, America's and England's gloominess. To avoid infringing upon any private life, the author has invented a small town, Verrieres, and when he needed a bishop, a jury, an assize court, he situated them all in Besancon, where has never been.

1. <u>LES MISERABLES</u> by Victor Hugo

2. <u>THE RED AND THE BLACK</u> by Stendhal

3. <u>MADAME BOVARY</u> by Gustave Flaubert

2

For many days we had been tempest-tossed. Six times had the darkness closed over a wild and terrific scene, and returning light as often brought but renewed distress, for the raging storm increased in fury until on the seventh day all hope was lost.

We were driven completely out of our course; no conjecture could be formed as to our whereabouts. The crew had lost heart and were utterly exhausted by incessant labor.

The river masts had gone by the board, leaks had been sprung in every direction. And the water, which rushed in, gained upon us...

* * *

...a thing it is when brethren dwell together in unity, under the eye of parental love."

Night has closed around me.

For the last time my united family slumbers beneath my care.

Tomorrow this closing chapter of my journey will pass into the hands of my eldest son.

From afar I greet thee, Europe!

I great thee, dear old *******!

Like thee, may New ******* flourish and prosper—good, happy, and free!

1. TWO YEARS BEFORE THE MAST by Richard Henry Dana, Jr.

2. SWISS FAMILY ROBINSON by Johann Rudolf Wyss

3. CAPTAINS COURAGEOUS by Rudyard Kipling

2

As no lady or gentleman, with any claims to polite breeding, can possibly sympathise with the ********* Family without being first assured of the extreme antiquity of the race, it is a great satisfaction to know that it undoubtedly descended in a direct line from Adam and Eve; and was, in the very earliest times, closely connected with the agricultural interest. If it should ever be urged by grudging and malicious persons, that a ******* in any period of the family history, displayed an overwhelming amount of family pride, surely the weakness will be considered not only pardonable but laudable, when the immense superiority of the house to the rest of mankind, in respect of this its ancient origin, is taken...

* * *

...spirit of that old man dead, who delighted to anticipate thy wants, and never ceased to honour thee, is there, among the rest: repeating, with a face composed and calm, the words he said to thee upon his bed, and blessing thee!

And coming from a garden, Tom, bestrewn with flowers by children's hands, thy sister, little Ruth, as light of foot and heart as in old days, sits down beside thee. From the Present, and the Past, with which she is so tenderly entwined in all they thoughts, thy strain soars onward to the Future. As it resounds within thee and without, the noble music, rolling round ye both, shots out the grosser prospect of an earthly parting, and uplifts ye both to Heaven!

1. <u>MARTIN CHUZZLEWIT</u> by Charles Dickens

2. <u>SWISS FAMILY ROBINSON</u> by Johann Rudolf Wyss

3. <u>PRIDE AND PREJUDICE</u> by Jane Austin

1

In the late summer of that year we lived in a house in a
a village across the river and the plain to the mountains. In the bed of the river there were pebbles and boulders, dry and white in the sun, and the water was clear and swiftly moving and blue in the channels. Troops went by the house and down the road and the dust they raised powdered the leaves of the trees. The trunks of the trees too were dusty and the leaves fell early that year and we saw the troops marching along the road then the dust rising and leaves, stirred by the breeze, falling and the soldiers marching and afterward the road bare and white except for the leaves.

* * *

"I do not want to talk about it," I said.

"I would like to take you to your hotel."

"No thank you."

He went down the hall. I went to door of the room.

"You can't come in now," one of the nurses said.

"Yes I can," I said.

"You can't come in yet."

"You get out," I said. "The other one too."

But after I had got them out and shut the door and turned off the light it wasn't any good. It was like saying good-by to a statue. After a while I went out and left the hospital and walked back to the hotel and the rain.

1. THE RED AND THE BLACK by Stendhal

2. A FAREWELL TO ARMS by Ernest Hemingway

3. THE RETURN OF THE NATIVE by Thomas Hardy

2

The writer, an old man with a white mustache, had some difficulty getting into bed. The windows of the house in which he lived were high and he wanted to look at the trees when he awoke in the morning. A carpenter came to fix the bed so that it would be on a level with the window.

Quite a fuss was made about the matter. The carpenter, who had been a soldier in the Civil War, came into the writer's room and sat down to talk of building a platform for the purpose of raising the bed. The writer had cigars lying about and the carpenter smoked.

For a time the two men talked...

* * *

...Helen White standing by a window in the ********* post office and putting a stamp on an envelope.

The young man's mind was carried away by his growing passion for dreams. One looking at him would not have thought him particularly sharp. With the recollection of little things occupying his mind he closed his eyes and leaned back in the car seat. He stayed that way for a long time and when he aroused himself and again looked out of the car window the town of ********* had disappeared and his life there had become but a background on which to paint the dreams of his manhood.

1. MAIN STREET by Sinclair Lewis

2. WINESBURG, OHIO by Sherwood Anderson

3. LOOK HOMEWARD, ANGEL by Thomas Wolfe

2

He was an inch, perhaps two, under six feet, powerfully built and he advanced straight at you with a slight stoop of the shoulders, head forward, and a fixed from-under stare which made you think of a charging bull. His voice was deep, loud, and his manner displayed a kind of dogged self-assertion which had nothing aggressive in it. It seemed a necessity, and it was directed apparently as much at himself as at anybody else. He was spotlessly neat, appareled in immaculate white from shoes to hat, and in the various Eastern ports where he got his living as ship-chandler's water-clerk he was very popular...

* * *

...when the reality of his existence comes to me with an immense, with an overwhelming force; and yet upon my honour there are moments, too, when he passes from my eyes like disembodied spirit astray amongst the passions of this earth, ready to surrender himself faithfully to the claim of his own world of shades.

"Who knows? He is gone, inscrutable at heart, and the poor girl is leading a sort of soundless, inert life in Stein's house. Stein has aged greatly of late. He feels it in himself, and says often that he is 'preparing to leave all this; preparing to leave...' while he waves his hand sadly at his butterflies."

1.
MOBY DICK by Herman Melville

2. LORD JIM by Joseph Conrad

3. CAPTAINS COURAGEOUS by Rudyard Kipling

2

General Miles with his gaudy uniform and spirited charge was the center for all eyes, especially as his steed was extremely restless. Just as the band passed the Commanding General, his horse stood upon his hind legs and was almost erect. General Miles instantly reined in the frightened animal and dug in his spurs in an endeavor to control the horse which, to the horror of the spectators, fell over backwards and landed squarely on the Commanding General. Much to the gratification of the people, General Miles was not injured but considerable skin was scraped off the flank of his horse. Almost every inch of General Miles's overcoat covered with the dust of the street and between the shoulders a hole about an inch in diameter was punctured. Without waiting for anyone...

* * *

...in a small arc when a car tears hissing past. Eyes seek the driver's eyes. A hundred miles down the road. Head swims, belly tightens, wants crawl over his skin like ants:

went to school, books said opportunity, ads promised speed, own your home, shine bigger than your neighbour, the radiocrooner whispered girls, ghosts of platinum girls coaxed from the screen, millions of winnings were chalked up on the boards in the offices, paychecks were for hands willing to work, the cleared desk of an executive with three telephones on it;

waits with swimming head, needs knot the belly, idle hands numb, beside the speeding traffic.

A hundred miles down the road.

1. <u>FINNEGAN'S WAKE</u> by James Joyce

2. <u>ALL QUIET ON THE WESTERN FRONT</u> by Erich Maria Remarque

3. <u>U. S. A. (Trilogy)</u> by John Dos Passos

3

Miss Brooke had that kind of beauty which seems to be thrown into relief by poor dress. Her hand and wrist were so finely formed that she could wear sleeves not less bare of style than those in which the blessed Virgin appeared to Italian painters; and her profile as well as her stature and bearing seemed to gain more dignity from her plain garments, which by the side of provincial fashion gave her the impressiveness of a fine quotation from the Bible—or from one of our elder poets—in a paragraph of today's newspaper. She was usually spoken of as being remarkably clever, but with the addition that her sister Celia had more common sense. Nevertheless, Celia wore scarcely more...

* * *

...of many Dorotheas, some of which may present a far sadder sacrifice than that of the Dorothea whose story we know.

Her finely touched spirit had still its fine issues, though they were not widely visible. Her full nature, like that river of which Cyrus broke the strength, spent itself in channels which had no great name on earth. But the effect of her being on those around her was incalcuably diffusive, for the effect of her being on those around her was incalculably diffusive, for the growing good of the world is partly dependent on unhistoric acts, and that things are not so ill with you and me as they might have been is half owing to the number who lived faithfully a hidden life rest in unvisited tombs.

1.
MIDDLEMARCH by George Eliot

2. ULYESSES by James Joyce

3. BUDDENBROOKS by Thomas Mann

1

From beyond the screen of bushes which surrounded the spring, Popeye watched the man drinking. A faint path led from the road to the spring. Popeye watched the man—a tall, thin man, hatless, in worn gray flannel trousers and carrying a tweed coat over his arm—emerge from the path and kneel to drink from the spring.

The spring welled up at the root of a beech tree and flowed away upon a bottom of whorled and waved sand. It was surrounded by a thick growth of cane and brier, of cypress and gum in which broken sunlight lay sourceless. Somewhere, hidden and secret yet nearby, a bird sang three notes and...

* * *

...she took out a compact and opened it upon a face in miniature sullen and discontented and sad. Bewide her father sat, his hands crossed on the head of his stick, the rigid bar of his moustache headed with moisture like frosted silver. She closed the compact and from beneath her smart new hat she seemed to follow with her eyes the waves of music, to dissolve into the dying brasses, across the pool and the opposite semicircle of trees where at somber intervals the dead tranquil queens in stained marble mused, on into the sky lying prone and vanquished in the embraced of the season of rain and death.

1. OF MICE AND MEN by John Steinbeck

2. ACROSS THE RIVER AND INTO THE TREES Ernest Hemingway

3. SANCTUARY by William Faulkner

3

On an evening in the latter part of May a middle-aged man was walking homeward from Shaston to the village of Marlott, in the adjoining Vale of Blakemore or Blackmoor. The pair of legs that carried him were rickety, and there was a bias in his gait which inclined him somewhat to the left of a straight line. He occasionally gave a smart nod, as if in confirmation of some opinion, though he was not thinking of anything in particular. An empty egg-basket was slung upon his arm, the nap of his hat was ruffled, a patch being quite worn away at its brim where his thumb came in talking it off. Presently he was met by an elderly parson astride on a gray mare, who, as he rode, hummed a wandering...

* * *

...of the tower a tall staff was fixed. Their eyes were riveted on it. A few minutes after the hour had struck something moved slowly up the staff, and extended itself upon the breeze. It was a black flag.

'Justice' was done, and the President of the Immortals, in Aescylean phrase, had ended his sport with *****. And the ********* knights and dames slept on in their tombs unknowing. The two speechless gazers bent themselves down to the earth, as if in prayer, and remained thus a long time, absolutely motionless: the flag continued to wave silently. As oon as they had strength they arose, joined hands again, and went on.

1. LES MISERABLES by Victor Hugo

2. TESS OF THE D'URBERVILLES by Thomas Hardy

3. BARCHESTER TOWERS by Anthony Trollope

2

It was late in the evening when K. arrived. The village was deep in snow. The ***** hill was hidden, veiled in mist and darkness, nor was there even a glimmer of light to show that a ****** was there. On the wooden bridge leading from the main road to the village, K. stood for a long time gazing into the illusory emptiness above him.

Then he went to find quarters for the night. The inn was still awake, and though the landlord could not provide a room and was upset by such a late and unexpected arrival, he was willing to let K. sleep on a bag of straw in the parlor...

* * *

"...I have no space for upstairs in my room, there I have two more wardrobes full, two wardrobes, each of them almost as big as this one. Are you amazed?"

"No, I was expecting something of the sort; didn't I say you're not only a landlady, you're aiming at something else?"

"I am only aiming at dressing beautifully, and you are either a fool or a child or a very wicked, dangerous person. Go, go away now!"

K. was already in the hall and Gerstacker was clutching at his sleeve again when the landlady shouted after him: "I am getting a new dress tomorrow, perhaps I shall send for you."

1. CRIME AND PUNISHMENT by Fyodor Dostoevski

2. BARCHESTER TOWERS by Anthony Trollope

3. THE CASTLE by Franz Kafka

3

He was an old man who fished alone in a skiff in the Gulf Stream and he had gone eighty-four days now without taking a fish. In the first forty days a boy had been with him. But after forty days without a fish the boy's parents had told him that the old man was now definitely and finally salao, which is the worst form of unlucky, and the boy had gone at their orders in another boat which caught three good fish the first week. It made the boy sad to see the old man come in each day with his skiff empty and he always went down to help im carry either the coiled lines or the gaff and harpoon and the sail that was furled...

* * *

...she asked a waiter and pointed to the long backbone of the great fish that was now just garbage waiting to go out with the tide.

"Tiburon," the waiter said. "Eshark." He was meaning to explain what happened.

"I didn't know sharks had such handsome, beautifully formed tails."

"I didn't either," her male companion said.

Up the road, in his shack, the old man was sleeping again. He was still sleeping on his face and the boy was sitting by him watching him. The old man was dreaming about the lions.

1. THE SEA WOLF by Jack London

2. CAPTAINS COURAGEOUS by Rudyard Kipling

3. THE OLD MAN AND THE SEA by Ernest Hemingway

3

Except for the Marabar Caves–and they are twenty miles off–the city of Chandrapore presents nothing extraordinary. Edged rather than washed by the river Ganges, it trails for a couple of miles along the bank, scarcely distinguishable from the rubbish it deposits so freely. There are no bathing-steps on the river front, as the Ganges happens not to be holy here; indeed there is no river front, and bazaars shut out the wide and shifting panorama of the stream. The streets are mean, the temples ineffective, and though a few fine houses exist they are hidden away in gardens or down alleys whose filth deters all but the invited...

* * *

...friends now?" said the other, holding him affectionately. "It's what I want. It's what you want."

But the horses didn't want it–they swerved apart; the earth didn't want it, sending up rocks through which riders must pass single file; the temples, the tank, the jail, the palace, the birds, the carrion, the Guest House, that came into view as they issued from the gap and saw Mau beneath: they didn't want it, they said in their hundred voices, "No, not yet," and the sky said, "No, not there."

1. LOST HORIZON by James Hilton

2. A PASSAGE TO INDIA by E. M. Forster

3. A RAZOR'S EDGE by William Somerset Maugham

2

With a single drop of ink for a mirror, the Egyptian sorcerer undertakes to reveal to any chance comer far-reaching visions of the past. This is what I undertake to do for you, reader. With this drop of ink at the end of my pen I will show you the roomy workshop of Mr. Jonathan Burge, carpenter and builder in the village of Hayslope, as it appeared on the eighteenth of June, in the year of our Lord 1799:

The afternoon sun was warm on the river workmen there, busy upon doors and window-frames and wainscoting. A scent of pine-wood from a tent-like pile of planks outside the open door mingled itself with the scent of elder-bushes which were spreading their summer snow..

* * *

...with her; and Lisbeth began to cry in the face of the very first person who told her se was getting young again.

Mr Joshua Rann, having a slight touch of rheumatism, did not join in the ringing of the bells this morning, and looking on some contempt at these informal greetings which required no official co-operation from the clerk, began to hum in his musical bass, 'O what a joyful thing it is,' by way of preluding a little to the effect he intended to produce in the wedding psalm next Sunday.

'That's a bit of good news to cheer Arthur,' said Mr Irwine to his mother as they drove off. 'I shall write to him the first thing when we get home.'

1. <u>BARCHESTER TOWERS</u> by Anthony Trollope

2. <u>ADAM BEDE</u> by George Elliot

3. <u>FAR FROM THE MADDING CROWD</u> by Thomas Hardy

2

Gil and I crossed the eastern divide about two by the sun. We pulled for a look at the little town in the big valley and the mountains on the other side, with the crest of the Sierra showing faintly beyond like the rim of a day moon. We didn't look as long as we do sometimes; after winter range, we were excited about getting back to town. When the horses had stopped trembling from the last climb, Gil took off his sombrero, the way he did when something was going to happen. We reigned to the right and went slowly down the steep stage road. It was a switch-back road, gutted by the...

* * *

...shootin'," Gil said.

"We've had enough of that," I told him.

"I know it," he said, "but I don't know how to start a decent fight with that kind of guy."

And then, like he was giving it a lot of attention, "He's a funny guy. I don't know how you'd start a decent fight with him."

Tink-tink-a-link went the meadow lark. And then another one, even farther off, teenk-teenk-a-leenk.

The Gil said, "I'll be glad to get out here," as if he's let it all go.

"Yeh," I said.

1. OF MICE AND MEN by John Steinbeck

2. THE OX-BOW INCIDENT by Walter Van Tilberg Clark

3. THE GRAPES OF WRATH by John Steinbeck

2

"I wonder when in the world you're going to do anything, Rudolf?" said my brother's wife.

"My dear Rose," I answered, laying down my eggspoon, "Why in the world should I do anything? My position is a comfortable one. I have an income nearly sufficient for my wants (no one's income is every sufficient, you know). I enjoy an enviable social position: I am brother to Lord Burlesdon, and brother-in-law to that most charming lady his countess. Behold it is enough!"

"You are nine-and-twenty," she observed, "and you've done..."

* * *

...Of that I know nothing; Fate has no hint, my heart no presentiment. I do not know. In this world, perhaps–nay it is likely–never. And can it be that somewhere, in a manner whereof our flesh-bound minds have no apprehension, she and I will be together again, with nothing to come between us, nothing to forbid our love? That I know not, nor wiser heads than mine. But if it be never–if I can never hold sweet converse again with her, or look upon her face, or know from her love why, then, this side the grave, I will live as becomes the man whom she loves; and for the other side I must pray a dreamless sleep.

1. THE PRISONER OF ZENDA by Anthony Hope

2. THE CASTLE by Franz Kafka

3. THE IDIOT by Fyodor Dostoevski

1

Dusk–of a summer night.

And the tall walls of the commercial heart of an American city of perhaps 400,000 inhabitants–such walls as in time may linger as a mere fable.

And up the broad street, now comparatively hushed, a little band of six,–a man about fifty, short, stout, with busy hair protruding from under a round black felt hat, a most important-looking person, who carried a small portable organ such as is customarily used by street preachers and singers. And with him a woman perhaps five years his junior, taller, not so broad, but solid of frame and vigorous, very plain in the face and dress, and yet not homely, leading...

* * *

...back"

"Yes, I will grandma, sure. You know me."

He took the dime that his Grandmother had extracted from a deep pocket in her dress and ran with it to the ice-cream vendor.

Her darling boy. The light and color of her declining years. She must be kind to him, more liberal with him, not restrain him too much, as maybe, maybe, she had–She looked affectionately and yet a little vacantly after him as he ran. "For his sake."

The small company, minus Russell, entered the yellow, unprepossessing door and disappeared.

1. MAIN STREET by Sinclair Lewis

2. U. S. A. (TRILOGY) by John Dos Passos

3. AN AMERICAN TRAGEDY by Theodore Dreiser

3

About thirty years ago, Miss Maria Ward of Huntingdon, with only seven thousand pounds, had the good luck to captivate Sir Thomas Bertram, of *************, in the county of Northampton, and to be thereby raised to the rank of baronet's lady, with all the comforts and consequences of a handsome house and large income. All Huntington exclaimed on the greatness of the match, and her uncle, the lawyer, himself, allowed her to be at least three thousands pounds short of any equitable claim to it. She had two sisters to be benefitted by her elevation; and such of their acquaintance as thought Miss Ward and Miss Frances quite as handsome as Miss Maria, did not scruple to predict their marrying with almost equal advantage. But there certainly...

* * *

...attached to country pleasures, their home was the home of affection and comfort; and to complete the picture of good, the acquisition of *********** living by the death of Dr. Grant, occurred just after they had been married long enough to being to want an increase of income, and feel their distance from the paternal abode an inconvenience.

On that event they removed to ********* and the parsonage there, which under each of its two former owners, Fanny had never been able to approach but with some painful sensation of restraint or alarm, soon grew as dear to her heart, and as thoroughly perfect in her eyes, as everything else, within the view and patronage of ********* had long been.

1. <u>BARCHESTER TOWERS</u> by Anthony Trollope

2. <u>WUTHERING HEIGHTS</u> by Emile Bronte

3. <u>MANSFIELD PARK</u> by Jane Austin

3

Cigars had burned low, and we were beginning to sample the disillusionment that usually afflicts old school friends who have met again as men and found themselves with less in common than they had believed they had. Rutherford wrote novels; Wyland was one of the Embassy secretaries; he had just given us dinner at Tempelhof–not very cheerfully, I fancied, but with the equanimity which a diplomat must always keep on tap for such occasions. It seemed likely that nothing but the fact of being three celibate Englishmen in a foreign capital could have brought us together, and I had...

* * *

...solemnly for a moment, and then answered in that funny clipped English that the educated Chinese have-'Oh, no, she was the most old-most old of any one I have ever seen.'

We sat for a long time in silence, and then talked again of Conway as I remembered him, boyish and gifted and full of charm, and of the War that had altered him, and of so many mysteries of time and age and of the mind, and of the little Manchu who had been "most old," and of the strange ultimate dream of Blue Moon. "Do you think he will ever find it?" I asked.

1. THE AMBASSADORS by Henry James

2. LOST HORIZON by James Hilton

3. TRISTAM SHANDY by Laurence Sterne

2

The story had held us, round the fire, sufficiently breathless, but except the obvious remark that it was gruesome, as, on Christmas Eve in an old house, a strange tale should essentially be, I remember no comment uttered till somebody happened to say that it was the only case he had met in which such a visitation had fallen on a child. The case, I may mention, was that of an apparition in just such an old house as had gathered us for the occassion- an appearance, of a dreadful kind, to a little boy sleeping in the room with his mother and waking her up in the terror of it; waking her not to dissipate his dead and soothe him...

* * *

...But he had already jerked straight round, stared, glared again, and seen but the quiet day. With the stroke of the loss I was so proud of he uttered the cry of a creature hurled over an abyss, and the grasp with which I recovered him might have been that of catching him in his fall. I caught him, yes, I held him–it may be imagined with what a passion; but at the end of a minute I began to feel what it truly was that I held. We were alone with the quiet day, and his little heart, dispossessed, had stopped.

1. THE TURN OF THE SCREW by Henry James

2. GREAT EXPECTATIONS by Charles Dickens

3. FRANKENSTEIN by Mary Shelley

1

The Nellie, a cruising yawl, swung to her anchor without a flutter of the sails, and was at rest. The flood had made, the wind was nearly calm, and being bound down the river, the only thing for it was to come to and wait for the turn of the tide.

The sea-reach of the Thames stretched before us like the beginning of an interminable waterway. In the offing the sea and the sky were welded together without a joint, and in the luminous space the tanned sails of the barges drifting up with the tide seemed to stand still in the red clusters of canvas sharply peaked, with gleams of varnished spirits. A haze rested on the low shores...

* * *

...have fallen, I wonder, if I had rendered Kurtz that justice which was his due? Hadn't he said he wanted only justice? But I couldn't. I could not tell her. It would have been too dark–too dark altogether..."

Marlow ceased, and sat apart, indistinct and silent, in the pose of a meditating Buddha. Nobody moved for a time. "We have lost the first of the ebb," said the Director suddenly. I raised my head. The offing was bared by a black bank of clouds, and the tranquil waterway leading to the uttermost ends of the earth flowed sombre under an overcast sky–seemed to lead into the heart an immense darkness.

1. CAPTAINS COURAGEOUS by Rudyard Kipling

2. HEART OF DARKNESS by Joseph Conrad

3. THE COUNT OF MONTE CRISTO by Alexander Dumas, Sr.

2

GILBERT MARTIN AND WIFE MAGDELANA (1776)

It was the second day of their journey to their first home. Lana, in the cart, looked back to see how her husband was making out with the cow. He had bought it from the Domine for a wedding present to her. He had hesitated a long while between the cow and the clock; and she had been disappointed when he finally decided on the cow, even thought it cost three dollars more; but now she admitted that it would be a fine thing to have a cow to milk. As he said, it would give her companionship when he was working in the woods.

Privately she had thought at the time that she would show him that she could manage their first house and help him with the fields also. She was a good strong girl, eighteen years old...

* * *

...his arm round Lana in the dark, leading her to the room they slept in. The baby was snuffling her breath in and out. As Lana started to unlace her short gown, she discovered the peacock's feather still in her hand. She fumbled for the shelf beside the window and laid the feather on it.

She heard Gil getting down on the bed; the rustle of straw beneath the blankets. Beyond the window the faintly clicking cowbells moved along the brook.

"We've got this place," she thought. "We've got the children. We've got each other. Nobody can take those things away. Not any more."

1. THE HOUSE OF THE SEVEN GABLES by Nathaniel Hawthorne

2. DRUMS ALONG THE MOHAWK by Walter Edmonds

3. SENSE AND SENSIBILITY by Jane Austin

2

The 25th day of August, 1751, about two in the afternoon, I, *************** came forth of the British Linen Company, a porter attending me with a bag of money, and some of the chief of these merchants bowing me from their doors. Two days before, and even so late as yestermorning, I was like a beggarman by the wayside, clad in rags, brought down to my last shillings, my companion a condemned traitor, a price set on my own head for a crime with the news of which the country rang. Today I was served heir to my position in life, a landed laird, a bank-porter by me carrying my gold, recommendations in my pocket, and (in the words of the saying) the ball directly at my foot...

* * *

As for ***** and Catriona, I shall watch you pretty close in the next days, and see if you are so bold as to be laughing at papa and mamma. It is true we were not so wise as we might have been, and made a great deal of sorrow out of nothing; but you will find as you grow up that even the artful Miss Barbara, and even the valiant Mr. Alan, will be not so very much wiser than their parents. For the life of man upon this world of ours is a funny business. They talk of angels weeping; but I think they must more often be holding their sides, as they look on; and there was one thing I determined to do when I began this long story, and that was to tell out everything as it befell.

1.
LORNA DOONE by Richard D. Blackmore

2. TOM JONES by Henry Fielding

3. DAVID BALFOUR by Robert Louis Stevenson

3

If anyone cares to read a simple told simply, I, John Ridd, of the parish of Oare, in the county of Somerset, yeoman and churchwarden, have seen and had a share in some doings of this neighbourhood, which I will try to set down in order, God sparing my life and memory. And they who light upon this book should bear in mind, not only that I write for the clearing of our parish from illfame and calumny, but also a thing which will, I trow, appear too often it, to wait–that I am nothing more than a plain unlettered man, not read in foreign languages, as a gentleman might be, nor gifted with long words (even in mine own tongue), save what I may have won from the Bible, or Master William Shakespeare, whom, in the face of common opinion, I do value highly. In short, I am an ignoramus,...

* * *

...More and more I hope, and think, that in the end he will win her; and I do not mean to dance again, except at dear Ruth's wedding, if a floor can found strong enough.

Of *****, of my lifelong darling, of my more and more loving wife, I will not talk; for it is not seemly, that a man should exalt his pride. Year by year, her beauty grows, with the growth of goodness, kindness and true happiness–above all with loving. For change, she makes of joke of this, and plays with it, and laughs at it; and then, when my slow nature marvels, back she comes to the earnest thing. And if I wish to pay her out for something very dreadful–as may happen once or twice, when we become too gladsome–I bring her to forgotten sadness, and to me for cure of it, by the two words, "*********."

1. LORNA DOONE by Richard D. Blackmore

2. MOLL FLANDERS by Daniel Defoe

3. JANE EYRE by Charlotte Bronte

1

In these times of ours, though concerning the exact year there is no need to be precise, a boat of dirty and disreputable appearance, with two figures in it, floated on the Thames, between Southwark Bridge which is of iron, and London Bridge which is of stone, as an autumn evening was closing in.

The figures in this boat were those of strong man with ragged grizzled hair and a sun-browned face, and a dark girl of nivneteen or twenty, sufficiently like him to be recognisable as his daughter. The girl rowed, pulling a pair of sculls very easily' the man, with the rudder-lines slack in his hands, and his hands loose in his waistband, kept an eager look-out. He had no net, hook, or line, and he could not be a...

* * *

...lady Tippins was never known to turn so very greedy, or so very cross. Mortimer Lightwood alone brightens. He has been asking himself, as to every other member of the Committee in turn, "I wonder whether you are the voice!" But he does not ask himself the question after Twemlow has spoken, and he glances in Twemlow's direction as if he were grateful. When the company disperse-by which time Mr. And Mrs. Veneering have had quite as much as they want of the honour, and the guests have had quite as much as they want of the other hounour–Mortimer sees Twemlow home, shakes hands with him cordially at parting, and fares to the Temple gaily.

1. OUR MUTUAL FRIEND by Charles Dickens

2. KIDNAPPED by Robert Louis Stevenson

3. PENDENNIS by William Makepeace Thackeray

1

On Friday noon, July the twentieth, 1714, the finest bridge in all Peru broke and precipitated five travellers into the gulf below. This bridge was on the high-road between Lima and Cuzco and hundreds of persons passed over it every day. It had been woven of osier by the Incas more than a century before and visitors to the city were always led out to see it. It was a mere ladder of thin slats swung out over the gorge, with handrails of dried vine, Horses and coaches and chairs had to go down hundreds of feet...

***

...Esteban and Pepita, but myself. Camila alone remembers her Uncle Pio and her son; this women, her mother. But soon we shall die and all memory of those five will have left the earth, and we ourselves shall be loved for a while and forgotten. But the love will have been enough; all those impulses of love return to the love that made them. Even memory is not necessarily for love. There is a land of the living and a land of the dead and the bridge is love, the only survival, the only meaning."

1. THE TOILERS OF THE SEA by Victor Hugo

2. TO THE LIGHTHOUSE by Virginia Woolf

3. THE BRIDGE OF SAN LUIS REY by Thornton Wilder

3

In Westphalia, in the castle of My Lord the Baron of Thunder-ten-Tronckh, there was a young man whom nature had endowed with the gentlest of characters. His face bespoke his soul. His judgement was rather sound and his mind of the simplest; this is the reason, I think, why he was named ***********. The old servants of the house suspected that he was the son of My Lord the Baron's sister and of a good and honorable gentleman of the neighborhood whom that lady never would marry because he could prove only seventy-one quarterings and the rest of his genealogical tree had been lost by the injuries of time.

My Lord the baron was one of the most powerful lords...

* * *

...an honest man. From time to time Pangloss would say to *********:

'There is a chain of events in this best of all possible worlds; for if you had not turned out of a beautiful mansion at the point of a jackboot for the love of Lady Caunegonde, and if you had not been involved in the Inquisition, and had not wandered over America on foot, and had not struck the Baron with your sword, and lost all those sheep you brought from Eldorado, you would not be here eating candied fruit and pistachio nuts.'

'That's true enough,' said *********; 'but we must go and work in the garden.'

1. CANDIDE by Voltaire

2. JUDE THE OBSCURE by Thomas Hardy

3. FATHER GORIOT by Honore de Balzac

1

On an exceptionally hot evening early in July a young man came out of the garret in which he lodged in S. Place and walked slowly, as though in hesitation, towards K. Bridge.

He had successfully avoided meeting his landlady, who provided him with garret, dinners, and attendance, lived on the floor below, and every time he went out he was obliged to pass her kitchen, the door of which invariably stood open. And each time he passed, the young man had a sick, frightened feeling, which made him scowl and feel ashamed. He was hopelessly in debt to his landlady, and was afraid...

* * *

...she was almost frightened of her happiness. Seven years, only seven years! At the beginning of their happiness at some moments they were both ready to look on those seven years as though they were seven days. He did not know that the new life would not be given him for nothing, that he would have to pay dearly for it, that it would cost him great striving, great suffering.

But that is the beginning of a new story–the story of the gradual renewal of a man, the story of his gradual regeneration, of his passing from one world into another, of his initiation into a new unknown life. That might be the subject of a new story, but our present story is ended.

1. BLEAK HOUSE by Charles Dickens

2. THE TRIAL by Franz Kafka

3. CRIME AND PUNISHMENT by Fyodor Dostoevski

3

Now that we are cool, he said, and regret that we hurt each other, I am not sorry that it happened. I deserved your reproach; a hundred times I have wished to tell you the whole story of my travels and adventures among the savages, and one of the reasons which prevented me was the fear that it would have an unfortunate effect on our friendship. That was precious, and I desired above everything to keep it. But I must think no more about that now. I must think only how I am to tell you my story. I will begin at a time when I was twenty-three. It was early in life to be in the thick of politics, and in trouble to the extent of having to fly my country to save...

* * *

...avail nothing, and there is no intercession, and outside of the soul there is no forgiveness in heaven and earth for sin. Nevertheless there is a way, which every soul can find out for itself–even the most rebellious, the most darkened with crime and tormented by remorse. In that way I have walked and, self-forgiven and self-absorbed, I know that if she were to return once more and appear to me–even here where her ashes are–I know that her divine eyes would no longer refuse to look ino mine, since the sorrow which seemed eternal and would have slain me to see would not now be in them.

1. REBECCA by Daphne du Maurier

2. CRIME AND PUNISHMENT by Fyodor Dostoevski

3. GREEN MANSIONS by W. H. Hudson

3

An Author ought to consider himself, not as Gentleman who gives a private or eleemosynary Treat, but rather as one who keeps a public Ordinary, at which all Persons are welcome for their Money. In the former Case, it is well known that the Entertainer provides what Fare he pleases; and tho' this should be very indifferent, and utterly disagreeable to the Taste of his Company, they must not find any Fault; nay, on the contrary, Good-Breeding forces them outwardly to approve and the command whatever is set before them. Now the contrary of this happens to be the Master of an Ordinary. Men who pay for what they eat, will insist on gratifying their Palates, however nice and whimsical these may prove; and if every Thing...

* * *

...Follies, acquired a Discretion and Prudence very uncommon in one of his lively Parts.

To conclude, as there are not to be found a worthier Man and Woman, than this found Couple, so neither can any be imagined more happy. They preserve the purest and tenderest Affection for each other, an Affection daily increased and confirmed b mutual Endearments, and mutual Esteem. Nor is their Conduct towards their Relations and Friends less amiable, than towards one another. And such is their Condescension, their Indulgence, and their Beneficence to those below them, that there is not a Neighbour, a Tenant, or a Servant, who doth not most gratefully bless the Day when Mr. ******* married to his Sophia.

1. TOM JONES by Henry Fielding

2. THE WAY OF ALL FLESH by Samuel Butler

3. THE PILGRIMS PROGRESS by Paul Bunyan

1

The rowdy gang of singers who sat at the scattered tables saw Arthur walk unsteadily to the head of the stairs, and though they must all have known that he was dead drunk, and seen the danger he would soon be in, no one attempted to talk to him and lead him back to his seat. With eleven pints of beer and seven small gins playing hide-and-seek inside his stomach he fell from the top-most stair to the bottom.

It was benefit Night for the White Horse Club, and the pub had burst its contribution box and spread a riot through its rooms and between its four walls. Floors shook and windows rattled, and leaves of aspidistras wilted in the fumes of beer and smoke. Notts County had beaten the visiting team and the members of the White Horse supporters club were quarted upstairs to receive a flow of victory. Arthur was not a member of the club, but Brenda was, and so he was drinking the share of her absent husband–as far it would go–and...

* * *

...into khaki at eighteen, and when they let you out, you sweat again in a factory, grabbing for an extra pint, doing women at the weekend and getting to know whose husbands are on the night-shift, working with rotten guts and an aching spine, and nothing for it but money to drag you back there every Monday morning.

Well, it's a good life and a good world, all said and done, if you don't weaken, and if you know that the big wide world hasn't heard from you yet, no, not by a long way, though it won't be long now.

The float bobbed more violently than before, and with a grin on his face, he began to wind in the reel.

1. <u>ULYSSES</u> by James Joyce

2. <u>ROOM AT THE TOP</u> by John Braine

3. <u>SATURDAY NIGHT AND SUNDAY MORNING</u> by Alan Sillitoe

3

The driver of the wagon swaying through forest and swamp of the Ohio wilderness was a ragged girl of fourteen. Her mother they had buried near the Monongahela–the girl herself had heaped with torn sods the grave beside the river of the beautiful name. Her father lay shrinking with fever on the floor of the wagonbox, and about him played her brothers and sisters, dirty brats, hilarious brats.

She halted at the fork in the grassy road, and the sick man quavered, "Emmy ye better turn down towards Cincinnati. If we could find your Uncle Ed, I guess he'd take us in."

"Nobody ain't going to take us in," she said. "We're going on jus' long as we can. Going West! They's a whole...

* * *

...Leora

That evening, after an unusually gay dinner with Latham Ireland, Joyce admitted, "Yes, if I do divorce him, I may marry you. I know! He's never going to see how egotistical it is to think he's the only man living who's always right!"

That evening, Martin *********** and Terry Wickett lolled in a clumsy boat, an extraordinarily uncomfortable boat, far out on the water.

"I feel as if I were really beginning to work now," said Martin. "This new quinine stuff may prove pretty good. We'll plug along on it for two or three years, and maybe we'll get something permanent–and probably we'll fail!"

1. <u>THE GRAPES OF WRATH</u> by John Steinbeck

2. <u>ARROWSMITH</u> by Sinclair Lewis

3. <u>WESTWARD HO!</u> by Charles Kingsley

2

The day had gone by just as days go by. I had killed it in accordance with my primitive and retiring way of life. I had worked for an hour or two and perused the pages of old books. I had had pains for two hours, as elderly people do. I had lain in a hot bath and absorbed its kindly warmth. Three times the mail had come with undesired letters and circulars to look through. I had done my breathing exercises, but found it convenient today to omit the thought exercises. I had been for an hour's walk and seen the loveliest feathery cloud patterns penciled against the sky. That was very delightful...

* * *

...exhausted, and ready to sleep for a whole year. I understood it all. I understood Pablo. I understood Mozart, and somewhere behind me I heard his ghastly laughter. I knew that all the hundred thousands pieces of life's game were in my pocket. A glimpse of its meaning had stirred my reason and I was determined to begin the game afresh. I would sample its tortures once more and shudder again at its senselessness. I would traverse not once more, but often, the hell of my inner being.

One day I would be a better hand at the game. One day I would learn how to laugh. Pablo was waiting for me, and Mozart too.

1. NAUSEA by Jean Paul Sartre

2. STEPPENWOLF by Hermann Hesse

3. GOODBYE MR. CHIPPS by James Hilton

2

riverrun, past Eve and Adam's, frm serve of shore to bend of bay, brings us by a commodius vicus of recirculation back to Howth Castle and Environs.

Sir Tristram, violer d;amores, fr;over the short sea, had passencore rearrived from North America on this side the scraggy isthmus of Europe Minor to wielderfight his penisolate war: nor had topswayer's rocks by the stream Oconee exaggerated themselve to Laurens County's gorgios while they went doublin their mumper all the time: nor avoice from afire bellowsed mishe mishe to tauftauf thuartpeatrick: not yet, though venisson after, had a kidscad buttended a bland old isaac: not yet, though all's fair in vanessy, were sosie sesthers wroth with twone...

* * *

...therrble prongs! Two more. Onetwo mormens more. So. Avelaval. My leaves have drifted from me. All. But one clings still. I'll bear it on me. To remind of. Lff! So soft this morning, ours. Yes. Carry me along, taddy, like you done through the toy fair! If I seen him bearing down on me now under whitespread wings like he'd come from Arkangels, I sink I'd die down over his feet, humbly dumbly, only to washup. Yes, tid. There's where. First. We pass through grass behush the bush to. Whish! A gull. Gulls. Far calls. Coming, far! End here. Us then. Finn, again! Take. Bussoflhee, mememormmee! Till thousendsthee. Lps. The keys to. Given! A way a lone a last a loved a long the

1. <u>FINNEGAN'S WAKE</u> by James Joyce

2. <u>ULYSSES</u> by James Joyce

3. <u>A PORTRAIT OF THE ARTIST AS A YOUNG MAN</u> by James Joyce

1

There is, as every schoolboy knows in this scientific age, a very close chemical relation between coal and diamonds. It is the reason, I believe, why some people allude to coal as "black diamonds." Both these commodities represent wealth; but coal is a much less portable form of property. There is, from that point of view, a deplorable lack of concentration in coal. Now, if a coalmine could be put into one's waist coast pocket–but it can't! At the same time, there is a fascination in coal, the supreme commodity of the age in which we are camp like bewildered travellers in a garish, unrestful hotel. And I suppose those two considerations, the...

* * *

...out. Wang was very pleased when he discovered him. That made everything safe, he said, and he went at once over the hill to fetch his Alfuro woman back to the hut."

Davidson took out his handkerchief to wipe the penetration off his forehead.

"And then, your Excellency, I went away. There was nothing to be done there."

"Clearly," assented the Excellency.

Davidson, thoughtful, seemed to weigh the matter in his mind, and then murmured with placid sadness:

"Nothing!"

1. SALAMMBO by Gustave Flaubert

2. VICTORY by Joseph Conrad

3. OMOO by Herman Melville

2

Petronius woke only about midday, and as usual greatly wearied. The evening before had been at one of Nero's feasts which was prolonged till late at night. For some time his health had been failing. He said himself that he woke up benumbled, as it were, and without power of collecting his thoughts. But the morning bath and careful kneading of the body by trained slaves hastened gradually the course of his slothful blood, roused him, quickened him, restored his strength, so that he issued from the elaeothesium, that is, the last division of the bath, as if he had risen from the dead, with eyes gleaming from wit and gladness, rejuvenated, filled with life, exquisite, so unapproachable that Ortho himself could not compare with him, and was relly that which he been called–arbiter elaganitarun.

He visited the public baths rarely, only when some rhetor...

* * *

...like a white flower. He placed it on the pillow to look at it once more. After that his veins were opened again.

At his signal the singers raised the song of Anacreon anew, and the citharae accompanied them so softly as not to drown as word. Petronius grew paler and paler; bt when the last sound had ceased, he turned to his guests again and said, – "Friends, confess that with us perishes–"

But he had not power to finish; his arm wth its last movement embraced Eunice, his head fell on the pillow, and he died.

The guests looking at those two white forms, which resembled two wonderful statues, understood well that with them perished all that was left to their world at that time, –poetry and beauty.

1. BEN HUR: THE TALE OF CHRIST by Lewis (Lew) Wallace

2. QUO VADIS by Henryk Sienkiewicz

3. ARABIAN NIGHTS by Princess Scherazade

2

Just after passing Caraher's saloon, on the County Road that ran south from Bonneville and that divided the Broderson ranch from that of Los Muertos, Presley was suddenly aware of the faint and prolonged blowing of a steam whistle that he knew must come from the railroad shops near the depot at Bonneville. In a starting out from the ranch house that morning, he had forgotten his watch, and was now perplexed to know whether the whistle was blowing for twelve or for one o'clock. He hoped the former. Early that morning he had decided to make a long excursion through the neighborhoring country, partly on foot and partly on bicycle, and now noon was come already, and as yet he had hardly.

* * *

...and shallow philanthropy of famine relief committees, the great harvest of Los Muertos rolled like a flood from the Sierras to the Himalays to feed thousands of starving scarecrows on the barren plains of India.

Falseness dies; injustice and oppression in the end of everything fade and vanish away. Greed, cruelty, selfishness, and inhumanity are short-lived; the individual suffers but the race goes on. Annixter dies, but in a far-distant corner of the world a thousand lives are saved. The larger view always and through all shams, all wickednesses, discovers the truth that will, in the end, prevail, and all things surely, inevitably, resistlessly work together for good.

1. THE OCTOPUS by Frank Norris

2. ARROWSMITH by Sinclair Lewis

3. HEAVEN'S MY DESTINATION by Thornton Wilder

1

The Rev. Septimus Harding was, a few years since, a beneficed clergyman residing in the cathedral town of *********; let us call it *************. Were we to name Wells or Salisbury, Exeter, Hereford, or Gloucester, it might be presumed that something personal was intended; and as this tale will refer mainly to the cathedral dignitaries of the town in question, we are anxious that no personality may be suspected. Let us presume that *********** is a quiet town in the West of England, more remarkable for the beauty of its cathedral and the antiquity of its monuments, than for any commercial prosperity; that the west end of *********** is the cathedral close, and that the aristocracy of ********* are the bishop, dean, and canons, with their respective wives.

* * *

...eighty he is never ill, and will probably die some day, as a spark goes out, gradually and without a struggle. Mr. Harding does dine with him very often, which means going to the palace at three and remaining till ten; and whenever he does not the bishop whines, and says that the port wine is corked, and complains that nobody attends to him, and frets himself off to bed an hour before his time.

It was long before the people of *********** forgot to call Mr. Harding by his long well-known name of *********. It had become so customary to say Mr. ***********, that is was not easily dropped. "No, no," he always says when so addressed, "not ***** no, only precentor."

1. <u>THE WARDEN</u> by Anthony Trollope

2. <u>RETURN OF THE NATIVE</u> by Thomas Hardy

3. <u>GOODBYE MR. CHIPS</u> by James Hilton

1

"Well, Piotr? Still nothing in sight?" asked a gentleman on the 20th of May, 1859, as he came out on the porch of the stage-coach inn on the road to–. Hatless, in a dusty overcoat and checked trousers, he looked a little over forty. He was addressed his servant, a chubby fellow with small, dim eyes and whitish fuzz on his chin.

Everything about the servant–his ingratiating suavity, his pomaded, varicolored hair, even his single turquoise earring–in short, everything distinguished him as belonging to the new, emancipated generation of servants. He looked down the road indulgently before answering, "No sir, still...

* * *

...words, brushing some dust off the stone, straightening a twig of the fir tree, they start to pray again and are unable to leave this pace in which they seem nearer to their son, to memories of him...But can their prayers, their tears be fruitless? Can love, holy, dedicated love not be all-powerful? Oh no! However passionate, sinful and rebellious the heart hidden in that grave may be, the flowers growing on it look at us undisturbed with their innocent eyes; they do not speak to us of eternal peace alone, of that supreme peace of the "impassive universe"; they also speak of eternal reconciliation and eternal life.

1. TARAS BULBA by Nickolai V. Gogal

2. THE BROTHERS KARAMOZOV by Fyodor Dostoevski

3. FATHERS AND SONS by Ivan Turgenev

3

It was love at first sight.

The first time Yossarian saw the chaplain he fell madly in love with him. Yossarian was in the hospital with a pain in his liver that fell just short of being jaundice. The doctors were puzzled by the fact that it wasn't quite jaundice. If it became jaundice they could treat it. If it didn't become jaundice and went away they could discharge him. But this just being short of jaundice all the time confused them.

Each morning they came around, three brisk and serious men with efficient mouths and inefficient eyes, accompanied by brisk and serious Nurse Duckett, one of...

* * *

...It won't be fun."

Yossarian started out. "Yes it will."

"I mean it, Yossarian. You'll have to keep on your toes every minute of every day. They'll bend heaven and earth to catch you."

"I'll keep on my toes every minute."

"You'll have to jump."

"I'll jump."

"Jump!" Major Daddy cried.

Yossarian jumped. Nately's whore was hiding just outside the door. The knife came down, missing him by inches, and he took off.

1. CATCH-22 by Joseph Heller

2. THE NAKED AND THE DEAD by Norman Mailer

3. THREE SOLDIERS by John Dos Passos

1

The year 1866 was marked by a strange occurrence, an unexplained and inexplicable phenomenon that surely no one has forgotten. People living along the coasts, and even far inland, had been perturbed by certain rumors, while seafaring men had been especially alarmed. Merchants, shipowners captains and skippers throughout Europe and America, naval officers of many nations, and governments on both continents-all were deeply concerned.

The fact was that for some time a number of ships had been encountering, on the high seas, "an enormous thing," described as a long, spindle-shaped object that was sometimes phosphorescent and infinitely larger and...

* * *

...is the case, if ************ still inhabits the ocean–his country of adoption–may all hatred have abated in his fierce heart! May the contemplation of so many marvels extinguish in him the spirit of vengeance! May the judge in him disappear, and may the scientist in him continue the peaceful exploration of the seal. However strange his destiny be, it also sublime. Did I not experience and understand his destiny? Did I not live that unnatural existence for ten whole months? So, to that question, asked six thousand years ago by the Book of Ecclesiastes: "Who has ever fathomed the depths of the abyss?" two men, among all men, have the right to reply: ********** and I.

1. SWISS FAMILY ROBINSON by Johann Rudolf Wyss

2. MOBY DICK by Herman Melville

3. TWENTY THOUSAND LEAGUES UNDER THE SEA by Jules Verne

3

"Eh bien, mon prince, so Genoa and Lucca are now no more than family estates of the Bonapartes. No, I warn you, if you don't say that this means war, if you still permit yourself to condone all the infamies, all the atrocities, of this Anti-Christ–and that's what I really he is–I will have nothing more to do with you, you are no longer my friend, my faithful slave, as you say. But how do you do, how do you do? I see that I am frightening you. Sit down and tell me all about it.

With these words the renowned Anna Pavlovna Scherer, lady-in-waiting and confidente to the Empress Marya Fyodorvna, greeted Prince Vasily, a man of high rank...

* * *

...of the Earth, but by admitting its immobility we arrive at an absurdity, while admitting its motion (which we do not feel) we arrive at laws," so in history the new view says: "It is true that we do not feel our dependence, but by admitting our free will we arrive at an absurdity, while by admitting our dependence on the external world, on time, on cause, we arrive at laws."

In te first case it was necessary to renounce the consciousness of an unreal immobility in space and to recognize a motion we did not feel; in the present case it is similarly necessary to renounce a freedom that does not exist, and to recognize a dependence of which we are not conscious

1. THE COUNT OF MONTE CRISTO by Alexander Dumas, Sr.

2. WAR AND PEACE by Count Leo Tolstoy

3. LES MISERABLES by Victor Hugo

2

On the 15th of September 1840, at six o'clock in the morning, the Ville-De-Montereau was lying alongside the Quai Saint-Bernard, ready to sail, with clouds of smoke pouring from its funnel.

People came hurrying up, out of breath, barrels, ropes and baskets of washing lay about in everybody's way; the sailors ignored all inquiries; people bumped into one another; the pile of baggage between the two paddlewheels grew higher and higher; and the din merged into the hissing of steam, which, escaping through some iron plates, wrapped the whole scene in a whitish mist, while the bell in the bows went on clanging incessantly...

* * *

...that he turned deathly pale, and stood still, without saying a word. The girls all burst out laughing, amused by his embarrassment; thinking they were making fun of him, he fled, and as Frederic had the money, Deslauriers had not choice but to follow him.

They were seen coming out. This caused a local scandal which was still remembered three years later.

They told one another the story at great length, each supplementing the other's recollections; and when they had finished:

'That was the happiest time we ever had,' said Frederic.

'Yes, perhaps you're right. That was the happiest time we ever had,' said Deslauriers.

1. A SENTIMENTAL EDUCATION by Gustave Flaubert

2. THE HUNCHBACK OF NOTRE DAME by Victor Hugo

3. THE COUNT OF MONTE CRISTO by Alexander Dumas Jr.

1

Strether's first question, when he reached the hotel, was about his friend; yet on his learning that Waymarsh was apparently not to arrive till evening he was not wholly disconcerted. A telegram from him bespeaking a room "only if not noisy," with the answer paid, was produced for inquirer at the office, so that the understanding that they should meet at Chester rather than at Liverpool remained to that extent sound. The same secret principle, however, that had prompted Strether not absolutely to desire Waymarsh's presence at the dock, that had led him thus to postpone for a few hours his enjoymnet of it, now operated to make him feel that he could still wait without disappointment...

* * *

...be so dreadfully right?

He considered, but he kept it straight. "That's the way that–if I must go–you yourself would be the first to want me. And I can't do anything else."

So then she had to take it, though still with her defeated protest. "It isn't so much your <u>being</u> 'right'–it's your horrible sharp eye for what makes you so."

"Oh, but you're just as bad yourself. You can't resist me when I point that out."

She sighed it at least all comically, all tragically, away."I can't indeed resist you."

"Then there we are!" said Strether.

1. <u>THE AMBASSADORS</u> by Henry James
2. <u>ULYSSES</u> by James Joyce
3. <u>THE PRISONER OF ZENDA</u> by Anthony Hope

1

A squat grey building of only thirty-four stories. Over the main entrance the words, CENTRAL LONDON HATCHERY AND CONDITIONING CENTRE, and, in a shield, the World State's motto, COMMUNITY, IDENTITY, STABILITY.

The enormous room on the ground floor faced towards the north. Cold for all the summer beyond the panes, for all the tropical heat of the room itself, a harsh thin light glared through the windows, hungrily seeking some draped lay figure, some pallid shape of academic goose-flesh, but finding only the glass and nickel and bleakly shining porcelain of a laboratory. Wintriness responded to wintriness. The overalls of the workers were white, their hands...

* * *

...no answer.

The door of the lighthouse was ajar. They pushed it open and walked into a shuttered twilight. Through an anarchy on the further side of the room they could see the bottom the staircase that led up to the higher floors. Just under the crown of the arch dangled a pair of feet.

"Mr. Savage!"

"Slowly, very slowly, like two unhurried compass needles, the feet turned towards the right; north, north-east, east, south-east, south, south-south-west; then paused, and, after a few seconds, turned as unhurriedly back towards the left. South-south-west, south, south-east, east...

1. <u>ANIMAL FARM</u> by George Orwell

<u>2. BRAVE NEW WORLD</u> by Aldous Huxley

3. <u>THE WAR OF THE WORLDS</u> by H. G. Wells

2

At the little town of Vevey, in Switzerland, there is a particularly comfortable hotel. There are, indeed, many hotels, for the entertainment of tourists is the business of the place, which, as many travelers will remember, is seated upon the edge of a remarkably blue lake–a lake that it behooves every tourist to visit. The shore of the lake presents an unbroken array of establishments of this order, of every category, from the "grand hotel" of the newest fashion, with a chalk-white front, a hundred balconies, and a dozen flags flying from its roof, to the little Swiss pension of an elder day, with its name inscribed in German-looking lettering upon a pink or...

* * *

...would have appreciated one's esteem."

"Is that a modest way?" asked Mrs. Costello, "of saying that she would have reciprocated one's affection?"

Winterbourne offered no answer to this question; but he presently said, "You were right in that remark that you made last summer. I was booked to make a mistake. I have lived too long in foreign parts."

Nevertheless, he went back to live at Geneva, whence there continue to come the most contradictory accounts of his motives of sojourn: a report that he is "studying" hard-an intimation that he is much interested in a very clever foreign lady.

1. BURDENBROOKS by Thomas Mann

2. TENDER IS THE NIGHT by F. Scott Fitzgerald

3. DAISY MILLER by Henry James

3

Buck did not read the newspapers, or he would have known that trouble was brewing, not alone for himself, but for every tidewater dog, strong of muscle and with warm, long hair, from Puget Sound to San Diego. Because men, groping in Arctic darkness, had found a yellow metal, and because steamship and transportation companies were booming the find, thousands of men were rushing into the Northland. These men wanted dogs, and the dogs they wanted were heavy dogs, with strong muscles by which to toil, and furry coats to protect them from the frost.

Buck lived at a big house in the sun-kissed...

* * *

...and passed him a fragment of a sea biscuit. He clutched at it avariciously, looked at it as a miser looks at gold, and thrust it into his shirt bosom. Similar were the donations from other grinning sailors.

The scientific men were discreet. They let him alone. But the privily examined his bunk. It was lined with hardtack; the mattress was stuffed with hardtrack; every nook and cranny was filled with hardtrack. Yet he was sane. He was taking precautions against another possible famine–that was all. He would recover from it, the scientific men said; and he did, ere the Bedford's anchor rumbled down in San Francisco Bay.

1. <u>TWO YEARS BEFORE THE MAST</u> by Richard Henry Dana, Jr.

2. <u>THE GRAPES OF WRATH</u> by John Steinbeck

3. <u>THE CALL OF THE WILD</u> by Jack London

3

In the latter days of July in the year 185-, a most important question for ten days hourly asked in the cathedral city of *********, and answered every hour in various ways–Who was to be the new bishop?

The death of old Dr. Grantly, who had for many years filled that chair with meek authority, took place exactly as the ministry of Lord *******was going to give place to that of Lord *******. The illness of the good old man was long as lingering, and it became at last a matter of intense interest to those concerned whether the new appointment should be made by a conservative or liberal government.

It was pretty well understood...

* * *

...reality they did no doubt receive advantage, spiritual as well as corporal, but this they could neither anticipate nor acknowledge.

It was a dull affair enough, this introduction of Mr. Quiverful, but still it had its effect. The good which Mr. Harding intended did not fall to the ground. All the ********** world, including the give old bedesmen, treated Mr. Quiverful with the more respect because mr. Harding had thus walked in, arm in arm with him, on his first entrance to his duties.

And here in their new abode we will leave Mr. And Mrs. Quiverful and their fourteen children. May they enjoy the good things which Providence has at length given to them!

1. OF HUMAN BONDAGE by William Somerset Maugham

2. BARCHESTER TOWERS by Anthony Trollope

3. CANDIDE by Voltaire

2

The little boy named Ulysses Macauley one day stood over the new gopher hole in the backyard of his house on Santa Clara Avenue in Ithaca, California. The gopher of this hole pushed up fresh moist dirt and peeked out at the boy, who was certainly a stranger but perhaps not an enemy. Before this miracle had been fully enjoyed by the boy, one of the birds of Ithaca flew into the old walnut tree in the backyard and after settling itself on a branch broke into rapture, moving the boy's fascination from the earth to the tree. Next, best of all, a freight train puffed and roared far away. The boy listened, and felt the earth beneath him trembe with the moving of the train...

* * *

...incredibly, the music began again–piano, harp, and the voices of three women.

"Let me stand here a moment and listen," the soldier said.

Ulysses came out of the house and took the soldier by the hand. When the song ended, Mrs. Macauley and Bess and Mary Arena came to the open door. The mother stood and looked at her two sons, one on each side of the stranger, the soldier who had known her son who was now dead. Stick to death, she nevertheless smiled at the soldier, and said, "Won't you please come in and elt us show you around the house?"

1. <u>THE HUMAN COMEDY</u> by William Saroyan

2. <u>TOM SAWYER</u> by Mark Twain

3. <u>ULYSSES</u> by James Joyce

1

It was the best of times, it was the worst of times, it was the age of wisdom, it was the age of foolishness, it was the epoch of belief, it was the epoch of incredulity, it was the season of Light, it was the season of Darkness, it was the spring of hope, it was the winter of despair, we had everything before us, we had nothing before us, we were all going direct to Heaven, we were all going direct the other way–in short, the period was so far like the present period, that some of its noisiest authorities insisted on its being received, for good or for evil, in the superlative degree of comparison only.

There were a king with a large jaw and a queen with a plain face, on the throne of England; there were a king...

* * *

...both

"I see that child who lay upon her bosom and who bore my name, a man winning his way up in that path of life which once was mine. I see him winning it so well, that my name is made illustrious there by the light of his. I see the blots I threw upon it, faded away. I see him, foremost of just judges and honoured men, bringing a boy of my name, with a forehead that I know and golden hair, to this place–then fair to look upon, with not a trace of this day's disfigurement–and I hear him tell the child my story, with a tender a faltering voice.

"It is far, far better thing that I do, than I have ever done; it is a far, far better rest that I go to, than I have ever known."

1. MOBY DICK by Herman Melville

2. A TALE OF TWO CITIES by Charles Dickens

3. THE PRINCE AND THE PAUPER by Mark Twain

2

On a hill by the Mississippi where Chippewas camped two generations ago, a girl stood in relief against the cornflower blue of Northern sky. She saw no Indians now; she saw flour-mills and the blinking windows of skyscrapers in Minneapolis and St. Paul. Nor was she thinking of squaws and portages, and the Yankee fur-traders whose shadows were all about her. She was meditating upon walnut fudge, the plays of Brieux, the reasons why heels run over, and the fact that the chemistry instructor had stared at her new coiffure which concealed her ears.

A breezae which had crossed a thousand miles of wheat-land belied her taffeta...

* * *

...this: I've never never excused my failures by sneering at my aspirations, by pretending to have gone beyond them. I do not admit that *********** is as beautiful as it should be! Id o not admit that Gopher Prairie is greater or more generous than Europe! I do not admit that dishwashing is enough to satisfy all women! I may not have fought the good fight, but I have kept the faith."

"Sure. You bet you have," said Kennicott. "Well, good night. Sort of feels to me like it might snow tomorrow. Have to be thinking about putting up the storm-windows pretty soon. Say, did you notice whether the central put that screwdriver back?"

1. MAIN STREET by Sinclair Lewis

2. SANCTUARY by William Faulkner

3. YOU CAN'T GO HOME AGAIN by Thomas Wolfe

1

The Salinas Valley is in Northern California. It is a long narrow swale between two ranges of mountains, and the Salinas River winds and twists up the center until it falls at last into Monterey Bay.

I remember my childhood names for grasses and secret flowers. I remember where a toad may live and what time the birds awaken in the summer–and what trees and seasons smelled like–how people looked and walked and smelled even. The memory of odors is very rich.

* * *

...Lee's face was haggard. He moved to the head of the bed and wiped the sick man's damp face with the edge of the sheet. He looked down at the closed eyes. Lee whispered, "Thank you, Adam–thank you, my friend. Can you move your lips? Make your lips form his name."

Adam looked up with sick weariness. His lips parted and failed and tried again. Then his lungs filled. He expelled the air and his lips combed the rushing sigh. His whispered word seemed to hang in the air.

"Timshell!"

His eyes closed and he slept.

1. EAST OF EDEN by John Steinbeck

2. CANNERY ROW by John Steinbeck

3. THE GRAPES OF WRATH by John Steinbeck

1

In the days when the spinning-wheels hummed busily in the farmhouses–and even great ladies, clothed in silk and thread-lace, had their toy spinning-wheels of polished oak-there might have been in districts far away among the lanes, or deep in the bosom of the hills, certain pallid undersized men, who, by the side of the brawny country-folk, looked like the remnants of a disinherited race. The shepherd's dog barked fiercely when one of these alien-looking men appeared on the upland, dark against the early winter sunset; for what dog likes a figure bent under a heavy bag?–and these pale men rarely stirred abroad without that mysterious burden.

* * *

...receive congratulations; not requiring the proposed interval of quiet at the Stone-pits before joining the company.

Eppie had a larger garden than she had ever expected there now; and in other ways there had been alterations at the expense of Mr. Cass, the landlord, to suit ****** larger family. For he and Eppie had declared that they would rather stay at the Stone-pits than go to any new home. The garden was fenced with stones on two sides, but in front there was an open fence, through which the flowers shone with answering gladness, as the four united people came within sight of them.

"O father," said Eppie, "what a pretty home ours is! I think nobody could be happier than we are."

1. SILAS MARNER by George Eliot

2. THE RETURN OF THE NATIVE by Thomas Hardy

3. SONS AND LOVERS by D. H. Lawrence

1

The stranger came early in February, one wintry day, through a biting wind and a driving snow, the last snowfall of the year, over the down, walking as it seemed from Bramblehurst railway station, and carried a little black portmanteau i his thickly gloved hand. He was wrapped up from head to foot, and the brim of his soft felt hat hid every inch of his face but the shiny tip of his nose; te snow had piled itself against his shoulders and chest, and added a white crest to the burden he carried. He staggered into the Coach and Horses, more dead than alive as it seemed, and flung his portmanteau down. "A fire," he cried, "in the name of human charity! A room...

* * *

...naked and pitiful on the ground, the bruised and broken body of a young man about thirty. His hair and beard were white–not grey with age, but white with the whiteness of albinism, and his eyes were like garnets. His hands were clenched, his eyes wide open, and his expression was one of anger and dismay.

"Cover his face!" said a man. "For Gawd's sake, cover that face!" and three little children, pushing forward through the crowd, were suddenly twisted round and sent packing off again.

Someone brought a sheet from the Jolly Cricketers, and having covered him, they carried him into that house.

1. THE WARDEN by Anthony Trollope

2. FOR WHOM THE BELLS TOLL by Ernest Hemingway

3. THE INVISIBLE MAN by H. G. Wells

3

The day broke grey and dull. The clouds hung heavily, and there was a rawness in the air that suggested snow. A woman servant came into a room in which a child was sleeping and drew the curtains. She glanced mechanically at the house opposite, a stucco house with a portico, and went to the child's bed.

'Wake up, Philip,' she said.

She pulled down the bed-clothes, took him in her arms, and carried him down-stairs. He was only half awake.

'Your mother wants you,' she said.

She opened the door of a room on the floor below and took the child over to a bed in which a woman was...

* * *

...you want to marry me?'

'There's no one else I would marry.'

'Then that settles it.'

'Mother and Dad will be surprised, won't they?'

'I'm so happy.'

'I want my lunch,' she said.

'Dear!'

He smiled and took her hand and pressed it. They got up and walked out of the gallery. They stood for a moment at the balustrade and looked at Trafalgar Square. Cabs and omnibuses hurried to and fro, and crowds passed, hastening in every direction, and the sun was shining.

1. OF HUMAN BONDAGE by William Somerset Maugham

2. GOODBYE, MR. CHIPS by James Hilton

3. TESS OF THE D'URBERVILLES by Thomas Hardy

1

The full truth of this odd matter is what the world has long been looking for, and public curiosity is sure to welcome. It so befell that I was intimately mingled with the last years and history of the house; and there does so live one man so able as myself to make these matters plain, or so desirous to narrate them faithfully. I knew the Master; on many secret steps of his career I have an authentic memoir in my hand; I sailed with him on his last journey almost alone; I made one upon that winter's journey of which so many tales have gone abroad; and I was there at the man's death. As for my late Lord Durrisdeer, I served him and loved him near twenty years; and thought more of him the more I knew of him. Altogether...

* * *

H.D.
HIS BROTHER
AFTER A LIFE OF UNLIMITED DISTRESS
BRAVELY SUPPORTED
DIED ALMOST IN THE SAME HOUR
AND SLEEPS IN THE SAME GRAVE
WITH HIS FRATERNAL ENEMY.
-
THE PIETY OF HIS WIFE AND ONE OLD
SERVANT RAISED THIS STONE
TO BOTH.

1. BLEAK HOUSE by Charles Dickens

2. THE MASTER OF BALLANTRAE by Robert Louis Stevenson

3. BARCHESTER TOWERS by Anthony Trollope

2

It was not long after dawn that Captain ********* came up on the quarterdeck of the Lydia. Bush, the first lieutenant, was officer on the watch, and touched his hat but did not speak to him; in a voyage which had by now lasted seven months without touching land he had learned something of his captain's likes and dislikes. During this first hour of the day the captain was not to be spoken to, nor his train of thought interrupted.

In accordance with standing orders–hallowed by now with the tradition which is likely to accumulate during a voyage of such incredible length–Brown the captain's coxswain, had seen to it that the weather side of the quarterdeck had been holystoned and sanded at the first peep of daylight. Bush and the midshipman with him withdrew.

* * *

...with the alliance of the Wellesley faction, but he could see with morbid clarity how often he would hate it; and he had been happy for thirty seconds with his son, and now, more morbidly still, he asked himself cynically if that happiness could endure for thirty years.

His eyes met Barbara's again, and he knew she was his for the asking. To those who did not know and understand, who thought there was romance his life when really it was the most prosaic of lives, that would be a romantic climax. She was smiling at him, and then he saw her lips tremble as she smiled. He remembered how Marie had said he was a man whom women loved easily,a nd he felt uncomfortable at being reminded of her.

1. CAPTAINS COURAGEOUS by Rudyard Kipling

2. THE SEA WOLF by Jack London

3. CAPTAIN HORATIO HORNBLOWER by C. S. Forester

3

We are at rest five miles behind the front. Yesterday we were relieved, and now our bellies are full of beef and haricot beans. We are satisfied and at peace. Each man has another mess-tin full for the evening; and, what is more, there is a double ration of sausage and bread. That puts a man in fine trim. We have not had such luck as this for a long time. The cook with his carroty head is begging us to eat; he beckons with his ladle to every one that passes, and spoons him out a great dollop. He does not see how he can empty his stewpot in time for coffee. Tjaden and Muller...

* * *

...know not. But so long as it is there it will seek its own way out, heedless of the will that is within me.

He fell in October 1918, on a day that was so quiet and still on the whole front, that the army report confined itself to the single sentence:
****

He had fallen forward and lay on the earth as though sleeping. Turning him over one saw that he could not have suffered long; his face had an expression of calm, as though almost glad the end had come.

1. THE RED BADGE OF COURAGE by Stephen Crane

2. A FAREWELL TO ARMS by Ernest Hemingway

3. ALL QUIET ON THE WESTERN FRONT by Erich Maria Remarque

3

In undertaking to describe the recent and strange incidents in our town till lately wrapped in uneventful obscurity, I find myself forced in absence of literary skill to begin my story far back, that is to say, with certain biographical details concerning that talented and highly-esteemed gentleman, Stepan Trofimovitch Verhovensky. I trust that these details may at least serve as an introduction, while my projected story itself will come later.

I will say at once that Sepan Trofimovitch had always filled a particular role among us, that of the progressive patriot, so to say, and he was passionately fond of playing the part–so much so that I really believe he...

* * *

...youth, have you stood nearer to a new and more terrible crime than at this moment."

"Calm yourself," Stavrogin begged him, positively alarmed for him. "Perhaps I will postpone... You're right...I will not publish the sheets. Compose yourself."

"No, not after the publication, but even before it, a day, an hour perhaps, before the great step, you will plunge into a new crime as a way out, and you will commit it solely to avoid the publication of these sheets, upon which you now insist."

Stavrogin veritably shook with anger and almost with fear.

"Cursed psychologist!" he suddenly cut the conversation short in a range, and, without looking back, left the cell.

1. THE POSSESSED by Fyodor Dostoevski

2. WAR AND PEACE by Count Leo Tolstoy

3. DEAD SOULS by Nikolai V. Gogol

1

I have never begun a novel with more misgiving. If I call it a novel it is only because I don't know what else to call it. I have little story to tell and I end neither with a death nor marriage. Death ends all things and so is the comprehensive conclusion of a story, but marriage finishes it very properly too and the sophisticated are ill-advised to sneer at what is by convention termed a happy ending. It is a sound instinct of the common people which persuades them that with this all that needs to be said is said. When male and female, after whatever vicissitudes you like, are at last brought together they have fulfilled their biological function and interest passes to the generation that is to come. But I leave my reader in the air. This book...

* * *

...was any way in which I could devise a more satisfactory ending; and to my intense surprise it dawned upon me that without in the least intending to I had written nothing more or less than a success story. For all the persons with whom I have been concerned got what they wanted: Elliot social eminence; Isable an assured position backed by substantial fortune in an active and cultured community; Gray a steady and lucrative job, with an office to go from nine till six every day; Suzanne Rouvier security; Sophie death; and Larry happiness. And however superciliously the highbrows carp, we the public in our heart of hears all like a success story; so perhaps my ending is not so unsatisfactory after all.

1. MAIN STREET by Sinclair Lewis

2. THE RAZOR'S EDGE by William Somerset Maugham

3. AN AMERICAN TRAGEDY by Theodore Dreiser

2

I wish either my father or my mother, or indeed both of them, as they were in duty both equally bound to it, had minded what they were about when they begot me; had they duly considered how much depended upon what they were then doing;–that not only the production of a rational Being was concerned in it, but that possibly the happy formation and temperature of his body, perhaps his genius and the very cast of his mind;–and, for aught they knew to the contrary, even the fortunes of his whole house ight take their turn from the humours and disposition which were then uppermost;–Had they duly weighed and considered all this, and proceeded accordingly,–I am very persuaded...

* * *

...as I am; said Obadiah.–Obadiah had not been shaved for three weeks–When–u---------u----------cried my father; beginning tbe sentence with an exclamatory whistle–and so, brother Toby, this poor Bull of mine, who is as good a Bull as ever p-issed, and might have done for Europa herself in purer tmes-had he but two legs less, might have driven into Doctors Commons and lost his character–which to a Town Bull, brother Toby, is the very same thing as his life–

L-rd! Said my mother, what is all this story about?-

A Cock and a Bull, said Yorick–And one of the best of its kind, I ever heard.

1. TRISTRAM SHANDY by Laurence Sterne

2. TOM JONES by Henry Fielding

3. CANDIDE by Voltaire

1

I had the story, bit by bit, from various people, and as generally happens in such cases, each time it was a different story. If you know Starkfield, Massachusetts, you know the post-office. If you know the post-office you must have seen ******** drive up to it, drop the reins on his hollow-backed bay and drag himself across the brick pavement to the white colonnade: and you must have asked who he was.

It was there that, several years ago, I saw him for the first time; and the sight pulled me up sharp. Even then he was the most striking figure...

* * *

...the bead-work table-cover, and went on with lowered voice: "There was one day, about a week after the accident, when they all thought Mattie couldn't live. Well, I say it's a pity she did. I said it right out to the minister once, he was shocked at me. Only he wasn't with me that morning when she first came to...And I say, if she's ha' died, ***** might ha' lived; and the way they are now, I don't see's there's much difference between the ***** up at the farm and the ***** down in the graveyard; 'cept that down there they're all quiet, and the women have got to hold their tongues."

1. THE SCARLET LETTER by Nathaniel Hawthorne

2. THE HOUSE OF SEVEN GABLES by Nathaniel Hawthorne

3. ETHAN FROME by Edith Wharton

3

The fourteenth of August was the day fixed upon for sailing of the brig Pilgrim on her voyage from Boston round Cape Horn to the western coast of North America. As she was to get under way early in the afternoon, I made my appearance on board at twelve o'clock, in full sea-rig, with my chest containing an outfit for a two or three years' voyage. I had undertaken this cruise to cure, if possible, by an entire change of life aby a long absence from books, a weakness of the eyes which had forced me to give up my studies.

The change from the tight frock coat, silk cap...

* * *

...others inquiring for friends on board or left upon the coast, and loafers in general.

Sail after sail, for the hundredth time, in fair weather and in foul, we furled now for the last time together. Then we came down to man the capstan, and with a chorus which awakened half of North End, we hauled the ship into the wharf.

The city bells were just ringing one when the last turn was made fast the crew dismissed. In five minutes more not a soul was left on board the good ship Alert but the old shipkeeper, who had come down from the counting-house to take charge of her.

1. CAPTAINS COURAGEOUS by Rudyard Kipling

2. CAPTAIN HORATIO HORNBLOWER by C. S. Forester

3. TWO YEARS BEFORE THE MAST by Richard Henry Dana, Jr.

3

The Jebel es Zubleh is a mountain fifty miles and more in length, and so narrow tat its tracery on the map gives it a likeness to a caterpillar crawling from the south to the north. Standing on its red-and-white cliffs, and looking off undert the path of the rising sun, one sees only the Desert of Arabia, where the east winds, so hateful to the vinegrowers of Jericho, have kept their playgrounds since the beginning. Its feet are well cvered by sands tossed from the Euphrates, there to lie; for the mountain is a wall to the pasture-lands of Moab and Ammon on the west–lands which else had been of the desert a part.

The Arab has impressed his language...

* * *

...Esther, what sayest thou?" asked **********

Esther came to his side, and put her hand on his arm, and answered:

"So wilt thou best serve the Christ. O my husbamd, let me not hinder, but go with thee and help."

*   *   *   *   *

If any of my readers, visiting Rome, will make the short journey to the Catacomb of San Calixto, which is more ancient than that of San Sebastiano, he will see what became of the fortune of **********, and give him thanks. Out of that vast tomb Christianity issued to supersede the Caesars.

1. <u>THE MARBLE FAUN</u> by Nathaniel Hawthorne

2. <u>EXODUS</u> by Leon Uris

3. <u>BEN HUR: A TALE OF THE CHRIST</u> by Lewis (Lew) Wallace

3

"The Bottoms" succeeded to "Hell Row". Hell Row was a block of thatched, bulging cottages that stood by the brookside on
Greenhill Lane. There lived the colliers who worked in the little gin-pits two fields away. The brook ran under the alder trees, scarcely soiled by these small mines, whose coal was drawn to the surface by donkeys that plodded wearily in a circle round a gin. And all over the countryside were these same pits, some of which had been worked in the time of Charles II, the few colliers and the donkeys burrowing down, like ants into the earth, making queer mounds and little black places among the corn-fields and the meadows. And the cottages of these coal-miners, in blocks and pairs...

* * *

...left them tiny and daunted. So much, and himself, infinitesimal, at the core a nothingness, and yet not nothing.

"Mother!" he whispered–"mother!"

She was the only thing that held him up, himself, amid all this. And she was gone, intermingled herself. He wanted her to touch him, have him alongside with her.

But no, he would not give in. Turning sharply, he walked towards the city's gold phosphorescence. His fists were shut, his mouth set fast. He would not take that direction, to the darkness, to follow her. He walked towards the faintly humming, glowing town, quickly.

1. SONS AND LOVERS by D. H. Lawrence

2. HOW GREEN WAS MY VALLEY by Richard Llewellyn

3. FAR FROM THE MADDING CROWD by Thomas Hardy

1

Late in the afternoon of a chilly day in February, two gentleman were sitting alone over their wine, in a well-furnished dining parlor, in the town of P******* in Kentucky. There were no servants present, and the gentleman, with chairs closely approaching, seemed to be discussing some subject with great earnestness.

For convenience sake, we have said, hitherto, two gentleman. One of the parties, however, when critically examined, did not seem, strictly speaking, to come under the species. He was a short, thick-set man, with coarse, common place features, and that swaggering air of pretension which marks a low man who is trying...

* * *

...the kingdom of Christ may come, can you forget that prophecy associates, in dread fellowship, the day of vengeance with the year of his redeemed?

A day of grace is held out to us. Both North and South have been guilty before God; and the Christian church has a heavy account to answer. Not by combining together, to protect injustice and cruelty, and making a common capital of sin, is this Union to be saved,–but by repentance, justice, and mercy; for, not surer is the eternal law by which the millstone sinks in the ocean, that the stronger law, by which injustice and cruelty shall bring on nations the wrath of Almighty God!

1. UNCLE TOM'S CABIN by Harriet Beecher Stowe

2. THE RED BADGE OF COURAGE by Stephen Crane

3. SANCTUARY by William Faulkner

1

In the time of Spanish rule, and for many years afterwards, the town of Sulaco–the luxurient beauty of the orange gardens bears witness to its antiquity–had never been commercially anything more important than a coasting port with a fairly large local trade in ox-hides and indigo. The clumsy deep-sea galleons of the conquerors that, needing a brisk gale to move at all, would lie becalmed, where your modern ship built on clipper lines forgers ahead by the mere flapping of her sails, had been barred out of Sulaco by the prevailing calms of its vast gulf. Some harbours of the earth are made difficult of access by the treachery of sunken rocks...

* * *

...into one great cry.

"Never! Gian' Battista!"

Dr. Monygham, pulling around in the police-galley, heard the name pass over his head. It was another of ******* triumphs, the greatest, the most enviable, the most sinister of all. In that true cry of undying passion that seemed to ring aloud from Punta Mala to Azuera and away to the bright line of the horizon, overhung by a big white cloud shining like a mass of solid silver, the genius of the magnificent Capataz de Cargadores dominated the dark gulf containing his conquests of treasures and love.

1. TREASURE ISLAND by Robert Louis Stevenson

2. NOSTROMO by Joseph Conrad

3. THE TOILERS OF THE SEA by Victor Hugo

2

********* was not beautiful, but men seldom realized it when caught by her charm as the Tarteton twins were. In her face were too sharply blended the delicate features of her mother, a Coast aristocrat of French descent, and the heavy ones of her florid Irish father. But it was an arresting face, pointed of chin, square of jaw, Her eyes were pale green without a touch of hazel, starred with bristly black lashes and slightly tilted at the ends. Above them, her thick black brows slanted upward, cutting a startling oblique line in her magnolia-white skin-that skin so prized by Southern women and so carefully guarded with bonnets, veils and mittens against hot...

* * *

...as she had wanted her when she was a little girl, wanted the broad bosom on which to lay her head, the gnarled black hand on her hair. Mammy, the last link with the old days.

With the spirit of her people who would not know defeat, even when it stared them in the face, she raised her chin. She could get ***** back. She knew she could. There had never been a man she couldn't get, once she set her mind upon him.

"I'll think of it all tomorrow, at *******. I can stand it then. Tomrorow, I'll think of some way to get him back. After all, tomorrow is another day."

1. THE SOUND AND THE FURY by William Faulkner

2. GONE WITH THE WIND by Margaret Mitchell

3. LOOK HOMEWARD, ANGEL by Thomas Wolfe

2

It was four o'clock when the ceremony was over and the carriages began to arrive. There had been a crowd following all the way, owning to the exuberance of Marija Berczynskas. The occasion rested heavily upon Marija's broad shoulders–it was her task to see that all things went in due form and after the best home traditions, and, flying wildly hither and thither, bowling everyone out of the way, and scolding and exhorting all day with her tremendous voice, Marija was too eager to see that others conformed to the properties to consider them herself. She had left the church last of all, and, desiring to arrive first at the hall, had issued orders to the coachman to drive faster. When that personage had developed a will...

***

...the greatest opportunity that has ever come to Socialism in America! We shall have the sham reformers self-stultified and self-convicted; we shall have the radical Democracy left without a lie with which to cover its nakedness! And then will begin the rush that will never be checked, the tide that will never turn till it has reached its flood–that will be irresistible, overwhelming–the rallying of the outraged workingmen of Chicago to our standard! And we shall organize them, we shall drill them, we shall marshall them for the victory! We shall bear down the opposition, we shall sweep it before us–and Chicago will be ours! Chicago will be ours! CHICAGO WILL BE OURS!"

1. SISTER CARRIE by Theodore Dreiser

2. THE AMERICAN by Henry James

3. THE JUNGLE by Upton Sinclair

3

On a brilliant day in May, in the year 1868, a gentleman was reclining at his ease on the great circular divan which at that period occupied the centre of the Salon Carre, in the Museum of the Louvre. This commodious ottoman has since been removed, to the extreme regret of all weak-kneed lovers of the fine arts; but the gentleman in question had taken serene possession of its softest spot, and, with his head thrown back and his legs outstretched, was staring at Murillo's beautiful moon-borne Madonna in profound enjoyment of his posture. He had removed his hat, and flung down beside him a little red guide-book and an opera-glass...

* * *

...assured her that there was nothing left of it.
"Well then," she said, "I suppose there is no harm in saying that you probably did not make them so uncomfortable. My impression would be that since, as you say, they defied you, it was because they believed that, after all, you would never really come to the point. Their confidence, after counsel taken of each other, was not in their innocence, nor in their talent for bluffing things off; it was in your remarkable good nature! You see they were right."

Newman instinctively turned to see if the little paper in fact consumed; but there was nothing left of it.

1. THE AMERICAN by Henry James

2. DAISY MILLER by Henry James

3. THE AMBASSADORS by Henry James

1

Jewel and I come up from the field, following the path in single file. Although I am fifteen ahead of him, anyone watching us from the cottonhouse can see Jewl's frayed and broken straw hat a full head above my own.

The path runs straight as a plumb-line, worn smooth by feet and baked brick-hard by July, between the green rows of laid-by cotton, to the cottonhouse in the center of the field, where it turns and circles the cottonhouse at four soft right angles and goes on across the field again, worn so by feet in fading precision...

* * *

...And then I see that the grip she was carrying was one of them little graphophones. It was for a fact, all shut up as pretty as a picture, and everytime a new record would come from the mail order and us setting in the house winter, listening to it, I would think what a shame Darl couldn't be to enjoy it too. But it is better so for him. This world is not his world; this life his life.

"It's Cash and Jewel and Vardaman and Dewey Dell," pa says, kind of hangdog and proud too, with his teeth and all, even if he wouldn't look at us. "Meet Mrs. Bundren" he says.

1. AS I LAY DYING by William Faulkner

2. THE WEB AND THE ROCK by Thomas Wolfe

3. THE RED BADGE OF COURAGE by Stephen Crane

1

Mr. Tench went out to look for his ether cylinder: out into the blazing Mexican sun and the bleaching dust. A few buzzards looked down from the roof with shabby indifference: he wasn't carrion yet. A faint feeling of rebellion stirred in Mr. Tench's heart, and he wrenched up a piece of the road with splintering finger-nails and tossed it feebly up at them. One them rose and flapped across the town: over the tiny plaza, over the bust of an ex-president, ex-general, ex-human being, over the two stalls which sold mineral water, towards the river and the sea. It wouldn't find anything there: the sharks looked after the carrion on that side. Mr. Tench went on across the plaza...

* * *

...pointed show got in the way.

The stranger said: "I have only just landed. I came up the river tonight. I thought perhaps.... I have an introduction for the Senora from a great friend of hers."

"She is asleep," the boy repeated

"If you would let me come in," the man said with an odd frightened smile, and suddenly lowering his voice he said to the boy: "I am a priest."

"You?" the boy exclaimed.

"Yes," he said gently. "My name is Father ---" but the boy had already swung the door open and put his lips to his hand before the other could give himself a name.

1. THE POWER AND THE GLORY by Graham Greene

2. THE BRIDGE OF SAN LUIS REY by Thornton Wilder

3. THE GRAPES OF WRATH by John Steinbeck

1

Dark spruce forest frowned on either side the frozen waterway. The trees had been stripped by a recent wind of their white covering of frost, and they seemed to lean toward each other, black and ominous, in the fading light. A vast silence reigned over the land. The land itself was a desolation, lifeless, without movement, so lone and cold that the spirit of it was not even that of sadness. There was a hint in it of laughter, but of a laughter more terrible than any sadness–a laughter that was mirthless as the smile of the Sphinx, a laughter cold as the frost and partaking of the grimness of infallibility. It was the masterful and incommunicable wisdom of eternity laughing...

* * *

...licked the ****** face.

Hand-clapping and pleased cries from the gods greeted the performance. He was surprised, and looked at them in a puzzled way. Then his weariness asserted itself, and he lay down, his ears *****, his head on one side, as he watched the *****. The other ***** came sprawling toward him, to ****** great disgust; and he gravely permitted them to clamber and tumble over him. At first, amid the applause of the gods, he betrayed a trifle of his old self-consciousness and awkwardness. This passed away as the *****' antic and mauling continued, and he lay with half-shut, patient eyes, drowsing in the sun.

1. THE CALL OF THE WIND by Jack London

2. WHITE FANG by Jack London

3. THE SEA WOLF by Jack London

2

A column of smoke rose thin and straight from the cabin chimney. The smoke was blue where it left the red of the clay. It trailed into the blue of the April sky and was no longer blue but gray. The boy Jody watched it, speculating. The fire on the kitchen hearth was dying down. His mother was hanging up pots and pans after the noon dinner. The day was Friday. She would sweep the floor with a broom of ti-ti and after that, if he were lucky, she would scrub it with the corn shucks scrub. If she scrubbed the floor she would not miss him until he had reached the Glen. He stood for a minute, balancing her hoe on his shoulder.

The clearing itself was pleasant if the unweeded...

* * *

...his moss pallet in the corner of the bedroom. He would never hear him again. He wondered if his mother had thrown dirt over Flag's carcass, or if the buzzards had cleaned it. Flag– he did not believe he should ever again love anything, man or woman or his own child, as he had loved ***********. He would be lonely all his life. But a man took it for his share and went on.

In the beginning of his sleep, he cried out, "Flag!"

It was not his own voice that called. It was a boy's voice. Somewhere beyond the sink-hole, past the magnolia, under the live oaks, a boy and *********** ran side by side, and were gone forever.

1. <u>THE YEARLING</u> by Marjorie Rawlings

2. <u>UNCLE TOM'S CABIN</u> by Harriet Beecher Stowe

3. <u>TOBACCO ROAD</u> by Erskine Caldwell

1

Halfway down a bystreet of one of our New England towns stands a rusty wooden house, with ************************* facing towards various points of the compass, and a huge, clustered chimney in the midst. The street is Pyncheon Street; the house is the old Pyncheon House; and an elm tree, of wide circumference, rooted before the door, is familiar to every town-born child by the title of the Pyncheon Elm. On my occasional visits to the town aforesaid, I seldom failed to turn down Pyncheon Street, for the sake of passing through the shadow of these two antiquities–the great elm tree and the weather-beaten ******

The aspect of the vulnerable mansion has always affected me like a human countenance, bearing the traces...

* * *

...of kaleidoscopic pictures in which a gifted eye might have foreshadowed the coming fortunes of Hepzibah and Clifford, and the descendant of the legendary wizard, and the village maiden, over whom he had thrown Love's web of sorcery. The Pyncheon Elm, moreover, with what foliage the September glare had spared to it, whispered unintelligible prophecies. And wise Uncle Venner, passing slowly from the ruinous porch, seemed to hear a strain of music, and fancied that sweet Alice Pyncheon–after witnessing these deeds, this bygone woe and this present happiness, of her kindred mortals–had given one fairwell touch of a spirit's joy upon her harpischord, as she floated heavenward from ***************.

1. <u>LITTLE WOMEN</u> by Louisa May Alcott

2. <u>THE HOUSE OF THE SEVEN GABLES</u> by Nathaniel Hawthorne

3. <u>THE BOSTONIANS</u> by Henry James

2

When I was a small boy at the beginning of the century I remember an old man who wore knee-breeches and worsted stockings, and who used to hobble about the street of our village with the help of a stick. He must have been getting on for eighty in the year 1807, earlier than which date I suppose I can hardly remember him, for I was born in 102. A few white locks hung about his ears, his shoulders were bent and his knees feeble, but he was still ale, and was much respected in our little world of Paleham. His name was Pontifex.

His wife was said to be his master; I have been told she brought him a little money but it cannot have been much. She was a tall, square-shouldered person (I have heard)...

* * *

...next generation rather than his own. He says he trusts that there is not, ad takes the sacrament duly once a year as a sop to Nemesis lest he should again feel strongly upon any subject. It rather fatigues him, but 'no man's opinions,' he sometimes says, 'can be worth holding unless he knows how to deny them easily and gracefully upon occasion in the cause of charity.' In politics he is a Conservative so far as his vote and interest are concerned. In all other respect he is an advanced Radical. His father and grandfather could probably no more understand his state of mind than they could understand Chinese, but those who know him intimately do not know that they wish him greatly different from what he actually is.

1. DAVID COPPERFIELD by Charles Dickens

2. THE WAY OF ALL FLESH by Samuel Butler

3. WAVERLY by Sir Walter Scott

2

Robert Cohen was once middleweight boxing champion of Princeton. Do not think that I am very much impressed by that as a boxing title, but it meant a lot to Cohen. He cared nothing for boxing, in fact he disliked it, but learned it painfully and thoroughly to counteract the feeling of inferiority and shyness he had felt on being treated as a Jew at Princeton. There was a certain inner comfort in knowing he could knock down anybody who was snotty to him, although, being very shy and throughly nice boy, he never fought except in the gym. He was Spider Kelly's star pupil. Spider Kelly taught all his young gentleman to box like featherweights, no matter whether they weighed one hundred and five or two hundred and five pounds.

* * *

...I tipped him and told the driver where todrive, and got in beside Brett. The driver started up the stret. I settled back. Brett moved closer to me. We sat close against each other. I put my arm around her and she rested against me comfortably. It was very hot and bright, and the houses looked sharply white. We turned out onto the Gran Via.

"Oh, Jake," Brett said, "we could have had such a damned good time together."

Ahead was a mounted policeman in khaki directing traffic. He raised his baton. The car slowed suddenly pressing Brett against me.

"Yes," I said. "Isn't it pretty to think so."

1. WINESBURG, OHIO by Sherwood Anderson

2. THE SUN ALSO RISES by Ernest Hemingway

3. TENDER IS THE NIGHT by F. Scott Fitzgerald

2

As I walked through the wilderness of this world, I lighted on a certain place was a den, and I laid me down in that place to sleep, and behold I saw a man clothed with rags, (Isaiah 64:6) standing in a certain place, with his face from his own house, a book in his hand, and a great burden upon his back. (Psalms 38:4) I looked, and saw him open the book, and read therein; and as he read he wept and trembled, and not being any longer to contain, be brake out with a lamentable cry, saying "What shall I do?" (Acts 16:30-31)

In this plight therefore he went home and refrained himself as long as he could that his wife and...

* * *

...and players on strings instruments, to welcome the ******* as they went up and followed one another in at the beautiful gate of that city.

As for Christian's children, the four boys that Christiana brought with her, with their wives and children, I did not stay where I was till they were gone over. Also since I came away I heard one say that they were yet alive, and so would be for the increase of the Church in that place where they were for a time.

Shall it be my lot to go that way again, I may give those that desire it an account of what I here am silent about; meantime I bid my reader adieu.

1. <u>THE PILGRIM'S PROGRESS</u> by Paul Bunyan

2. <u>THE HEART OF MIDLOTHIAN</u> by Sir Walter Scott

3. <u>JUDE THE OBSCURE</u> by Thomas Hardy

1

At eight o'clock in the inner vestibule of the Auditorium Theatre by the window of the box office, Laura Dearborn, her younger sister Page, and their aunt–Aunt Wess–were still waiting for the rest of the theatre-party to appear. A great, slow moving press of men and women in evening dress filled the vestibule from one wall to another. A confused murmur of talk and the shuffling of many feet arose on all sides, while from time to time, when the outside and inside doors of the entrance chanced to be open simultaneously, a sudden draught of air gushed in, damp, glacial, and edged with the penetrating keenness...

* * *

...haze of light, and silhouetted against this rose a sombre mass, unbroken by any glimmer, rearing a black and formidable facade against the blur of the sky behind it.

And this was the last impression of the part of her life that the day brought to a close: the tall gray office buildings, the murk of rain, the haze of light in the heavens, and raised against it, the pile of the Board of Trade building, black, monolithic, crouching on its foundations like a monstrous sphinx with blind eyes, silent, grave–crouching there without a sound, without sign of life, under the night and drifting veil of rain.

1. MAIN STREET by Sinclair Lewis

2. THE PIT by Frank Norris

3. AN AMERICAN TRAGEDY by Theodore Dreiser

2

My father's family name being Pirrip, and my Christian name Phillip, my infant tongue could make of both names nothing longer or more explicit than Pip. So, I called myself Pip, and came to be called Pip.

I gave Pirrip as my father's family name, on the authority of his tombstone and my sister - Mrs Joe Gargery, who married the blacksmith. As I never saw my father or my mother, and never saw any likeness of either of them (for their days were long before the days of photographs), my first fancies regarding what they were like, were unreasonably derived from their tombstones. The shape of the letters on my father's gave me an odd idea that he was a square, stout, dark man, with curly black hair. From...

* * *

...has been stronger than all other teaching, and has taught me to understand what your heart used to be. I have been bent and broken, but - I hope - into a better shape. Be as considerate and good to me as you were, and tell me we are friends.'

'We are friends,' said I, rising and bending over her, as she rose from the bench.

'And will continue friends apart,' said Estella.

I took her hand in mine, and we went out of the ruined place' and, as the morning mists had risen long ago when I first left the forge, so, the evening mists were rising now, and in all the broad expanse of tranquil light they showed to me, I saw no shadow of another parting from her.

1. THE RETURN OF THE NATIVE by Thomas Hardy

2. THE RED AND THE BLACK by Stendhal

3. GREAT EXPECTATIONS by Charles Dickens

3

He sat, in defiance of municipal orders, astride the gun Zam-Zammah on her brick platform opposite the old Ajaib-Gher–the Wonder House, as the natives call the Lahore Museum. Who hold Zam-Zammah, that "fire-breathing dragon," hold the Punjab, for the great green-bronze piece is always first of the conquerer's loot.

There was some justification for ***** - he had hicked Lala Dinanath's boy off the trunnions, –since the Englush held the Punjab and ***** was English. Though he was burned black as any native; though he spoke the vernacular by preference, and his mother-tongue in a clipped uncertain sing-song; though he consorted on terms of perfect equality with the...

* * *

...from the North with a cot and men, and they put the body on the cot and bore it up to the Sabiba's house."

"What said the Sahiba?"

"I was meditating in that body, and did not hear. So thus the Search is ended. For the merit that I have acquired, the River of the Arrow is here. It broke forth at our feet, as I have said. I have found it. Son of my Soul. I have wrenched my Soul back from the Threshold of Freedom to free thee from all sin–as I am free, and sinless. Just is the Wheel! Certain is our deliverance. Come!"

He crossed his hands on his lap and smiled, as a man may who has won salvation for himself and his beloved.

1. A PASSAGE TO INDIA by E. M. Forster

2. LORD JIM by Joseph Conrad

3. KIM by Rudyard Kipling

3

The cold passed reluctantly from the earth, and the retiring fogs revealed an army stretched out on the hills, resting. As the landscape changed from brown to green, the army awakened, and began to tremble with eagerness at the noise of rumors. It cast its eyes upon the roads, which were growing from long troughs of liquid mud to proper throughfares. A river, ambertinted in the shadow of its banks purled at the army's feet; and at night, when the stream had become of a sorrowful blackness, one could see across it the red, eyelike gleam of hostile camp fires set in the low brows of distant...

* * *

...churning effort in a trough of liquid brown mud under a low, wretched sky. Yet the youth smiled, for he saw that the world was a world for him, though many discovered it to be made of oaths and walking sticks. He had rid himself of the sickness of ******. The sultry nightmare was in the past. He had been an animal blistered and sweating in the heat and pain of war. He turned now with a lover's thirst to images of tranquil skies, fresh meadows, cool brooks–an existence of soft and eternal peace.

Over the river a golden ray of sun came through the hosts of leaden rain clouds.

1. <u>THE NAKED AND THE DEAD</u> by Norman Mailer

2. <u>THE RED BADGE OF COURAGE</u> by Stephen Crane

3. <u>ALL QUIET ON THE WESTERN FRONT</u> by Erich Maria Remarque

2

The weather door of the smoking-room had been left open to the North Atlantic fog, as the big liner rolled and lifted, whistling to warn the fishing-fleet. "That Cheyne boy's the biggest nuisance aboard," said a man in a freize overcoat, shutting the door with a bang. "He isn't wanted her. He's too fresh."

A white-haired German reached for a sandwich, and grunted between bites. "I know der breed. Ameriga is full of dot kind. I dell you should imbort ropes' end free under.

* * *

...coal-black Celt with the second-sight did not see fit to reply till he had tapped Dan on the shoulder, and for the twentieth time croaked the old, old prophecy in his ear.

"Master-man. Man-master," said he. "You remember, Dan Troop, what I said? On the <u>We're Here?</u>"

"Well, I won't go so far as to deny that it do look like it as things stand at present," said Dan.

"She was a noble packet, and one way an' another I owe her a heap–her and Dad."

"Me too," quoth Harvey Cheyne.

1. <u>CAPTAINS COURAGEOUS</u> by Rudyard Kipling

2. <u>TWO YEARS BEFORE THE MAST</u> by Richard Henry Dana, Jr.

3. <u>CAPTAIN HORATIO HORNBLOWER</u> by C. S. Forester

1

Although I am an old man, night is generally my time for walking. In the summer I often leave home early in the morning, and roam about the fields and lanes all day, or even escape for days or weeks together; but, saving in the country, I seldom go out until after dark, though, Heaven be thanked, I love its light and feel the cheerfulness t sheds upon the earth, as much as any living living.

I have fallen insensibly into this habit, both because it favours my infirmity, and because it affords me greater opportunity of speculating on the characters and occupations of those who fill the streets. The glare and hurry of broad noon are not adapted to idle pursuits like mine; a glimpse.

***

...tears, and laugh themselves to think that she had done so, and be again quite merry.

He sometimes took tem to the street where she had lived; but new improvements had altered it so much, it was not like the same. The old house had been long ago pulled down, and a fine broad road was in its place. At first he would draw with his stick a square upn the ground to show them where it used to stand. But, he soon became uncertain of the spot, and could only say it was thereabouts, he thought, and these alterations were confusing.

Such are the changes which a few years bring about, and so do things pass away, like a tale that is told!

1. THE OLD MAN AND THE SEA by Ernest Hemingway

2. THE VICAR OF WAKEFIELD by Oliver Goldsmith

3. THE OLD CURIOSITY SHOP by Charles Dickens

3

Call me Ishmael. Some years ago–never mind how long precisely–having little or no money in my purse, and nothing particular to interest me on shore, I thought I would sail about a little and see the watery part of the world. It is a way I have of driving off the spleen, and regulating the circulation. Whenever I find myself growing grim about the mouth; whenever it is a damp, drizzly November in my soul; whenever I find myself involuntarily pausing before coffin warehouses, and bringing up the rear of every funeral I meet; and especially whenever my hypos get such an upper hand of me, that it requires a strong moral principle to prevent me from deliberately...

* * *

...hammer and the wood; and simultaneously feeling that ethereal thrill, the submerged savage beneath, in his death-gasp, kept his hammer frozen there; and so the bird of heaven, with archangelic shrieks, and his imperial beak thrust upwards, and his whole captive form folded in the flag of *****, went down with the ship, which like Satan, would not sink to hell till she had dragged a living part of heaven along with her, and helmeted herself with it.

Now small fowls flew screaming over the yet yawning gulf; a sullen white surf beat against its steep sides; then all collapsed, and the great shrould of the sea rolled on as it rolled five thousand years before.

1. <u>THE SEA WOLF</u> by Jack London

2. <u>MOBY DICK</u> by Herman Melville

3. <u>CAPTAINS COURAGEOUS</u> by Rudyard Kipling

2

It was **************** marriage day. At first, opening his eyes in the blackness of the curtains about his bed, he could not think why the dawn seemed different from any other. The house was still except for the faint, gasping cough of his old father, whose room was opposite to his own across the middle room. Every morning the old man's cough was the first sound to be heard. ********* usually lay listening to it and moved only when he heard it approaching nearer and when he heard the door of his father's room squeak upon its wooden hinges.

But this morning he did not wait. He sprang up and pushed aside the curtains of his bed. It was dark, ruddy dawn, and though a small square hole of a window, where the...

* * *

...And the old man let his scanty tears dry upon his cheeks and they made salty stains there. And he stooped and took up a handful of the soil and he held it and he muttered,

"If you sell the land, it is the end."

And his two sons held him, one on either side, each holding his arm, and he held tight in his hand the warm loose earth. And they sooted him and they said over and over, the eldest son and the second son,

"Rest assured, our father, rest assured. The land is not to be sold." But over the old man's head they looked at each and smiled.

1. <u>THE GOOD EARTH</u> by Pearl Buck

2. <u>TOBACCO ROAD</u> by Erskine Caldwell

3. <u>THE MASTER OF BALLANTRAE</u> by Robert Louis Stevenson

1

Though I haven't ever been on the screen I was brought up in pictures. Rudolph Valentino came to my fifth birthday party–or so I was told. I put this down only to indicate that even before the age of reason I was in a position to watch the wheels go round.

I was going to write my memoirs once, The Producer's Daughter, but at eighteen you never quite get around to anything like that. It's just as well–it would have been as flat as an old column of Lolly Parsons'. My father was in the picture business as another man might be in cotton or steel, and I took it tranquilly. At the worst I accepted ******* with the resignation of a ghost assigned to a haunted house.

* * *

...a result of the death of Stahr and the murder of her father she now breaks down completely. She develops tuberculosis, and we were to learn for the first time at the end that she has been putting together her story in a tuberculosis sanitarium. (See the first of the fragments under Cecilia.)

We were to have had a final picture of Kathleen standing outside the studio. She has presumably separated from her husband as a result of the plot against Stahr. It had been one of her chief attracts for Stahr that she did not belong to the Hollywood world; and now she knows that she is never to be part of it. She is always to remain on the outside of tings–a situation which also has its tragedy.

1. THE LAST TYCOON by F. Scott Fitzgerald

2. AN AMERICAN TRAGEDY by Theodore Dreiser

3. ARROWSMITH by Sinclair Lewis

1

"The time has now come for me to hear a step in the passage," said Bernard to himself. He raised his head and listened. Nothing! His father and elder brother were away at the law-courts; his mother paying visits; his sister at a concert; as for his small brother Caloub–the youngest–he was safely shut up for the whole afternoon in his day-school. Bernard Profitendieu had stayed at home to cram for his "bachot", he had only three more weeks before him. His family respected his solitude–not so the demon! Although Bernard had stripped off his coat, he was stifling. The window that looked on to the street stood open, but it let in nothing but heat. His forehead was streaming. A drop of perspiration came dripping from his nose...

* * *

...which George had passed him and which he had flicked away with his finger, was found later under a bench and also contributed to help him. True, he remained guilty, as did George and Phiphi, of having lent himself to a cruel game, but he would not have done so, he declared, if he had thought the weapon was loaded. George was the only one who remained convinced his entire responsibility.

George was not so corrupted but that his admiration for Gheridanisol yielded at last to horror. When he reached home that evening, he flunt himself into his mother's arms; and Pauline had a burst of gratitude to God, who by means of this dreadful tragedy had brought her son back to her.

1. THE COUNTERFEITERS by Andre Gide

2. EUGENIE GRANDET by Honore de Balzac

3. CAMILLE by Alexander Dumas Jr.

1

On February 24, 1815, the watchtower at Marseilles signaled the arrival of the three-master Pharaon, coming from Smyrna, Trieste and Naples.

The quay was soon covered with the usual crowd of curious onlookers, for the arrival of a ship is always a great event in Marseilles, especially when, like the Pharaon, it has been built, rigged and laden in the city and belongs to a local shipowner.

Meanwhile the vessel was approaching the harbor under topsails, jib and foresail, but so slowly and with such an air of melancholy that the onlookers, instinctively sensing misfortune, began to wonder what accident could have happened on board. However, the experienced seamen...

* * *

...said Jacopo.

The two young people looked in the direction in which he was pointing. On the dark blue line separating the sky from the Mediterranean they saw a white sail.

"Gone!" cried Maximilien. "Farewell, my friend, my father!"

"Gone!" murmured Valentine. "Farwell, my friend! Farewell my sister!"

"Who knows if we'll ever see them again?" said Maximilien.

"My darling," said Valentine, "the count just told us that all human wisdom was contained in these two words: Wait and hope."

1. A SENTIMENTAL EDUCATION by Gustave Flaubert

2. THE COUNT OF MONTE CRISTO by Alexander Dumas Sr.

3. THE HUNCHBACK OF NOTRE DAME by Victor Hugo

2

Now what I want is Facts. Teach these boys and girls nothing but Facts. Facts alone are wanted in life. Plant nothing else, and root out everything else. You can only form the minds of reasoning animals upon Facts: nothing else will ever be of any service to them. This is the principle on which I bring up my own children, and this is the principle on which I bring up these children. Stick to Facts, sir!"

***

...will wither up, the sturdiest physical manhood will be morally stark death, and the plainest national prosperity figures can show will be the Writing on the Wall–she holding this course as part of a no fantastic vow, or bond, or brotherhood, or sisterhood, or pledge, or covenant, or fancy dress, or fancy fair, but simply as a duty to be done–did Louisa see these things of herself? These things were to be.

Dear reader! It rests with you and ne whether, in our two fields of action, similar things shall be or not. Let them be! We shall sit with lighter bosoms on the hearth, to see the ashes of our fires turn grey and cold.

1. HARD TIMES by Charles Dickens

2. TESS OF THE D'URBERVILLES by Thomas Hardy

3. PRIDE AND PREJUDICE by Jane Austin

1

You will rejoice to hear that no disaster has accompanied the commencement of an enterprise which you have regarded with such evil forebodings. I arrived here yesterday, and my first task is to assure my dear sister of my welfare and increasing confidence in the success of my undertaking.

I am already far north of London, and as I walk in the streets of Petersburgh, I feel a cold northern breeze play upon my cheeks, which braces my nerves and fills me with delight. Do you understand this feeling? This breeze, which has travelled from the regions towards which I am advancing, gives me a foretaste of those icy...

* * *

...he cried with sad and solemn enthusiasm, "I shall die, and what I now feel be no longer felt. Soon those burning miseries will be extinct. I shall ascend my funeral pile triumphantly and exult in the agony of the torturing flames. The light of that configuration will fade away; my ashes will be swept into the sea by the winds. My spirit will sleep in peace, or if it thinks, it will not surely think thus. Farewell."

He sprang from the cabin window as he said this, upon the ice raft which lay close to the vessel. He was soon borne away by the waves and lost in darkness and distance.

1. FRANKENSTEIN by Mary Shelley

2. LOST HORIZON by James Hilton

3. THE IDIOT by Fyodor Dostoevski

1

I have noticed that when someone asks for you on the telephone and, finding you out, leaves a message begging you to call him up the moment you come in, as it's important, the matter is more often important to him than to you. When it comes to making you a present or doing you a favor most people are able to hold their impatience with reasonable bounds. So when I got back to my lodgings with just enough time to have a drink a cigarette, and to read my paper before dressing for dinner, and was told by Miss Fellows, my landlady, that Mr. Alroy Kear wished me to ring him up at once, I felt that I could safely ignore his request.

'Is that the writer?' she asked.

***

...soon after his arrival in America; perhaps at the time of their marriage. It was a three-quarter length. It showed him in a long frock-coat, tightly buttoned, and a tall silk hat cocked rakishly on one side of his head; there was a large rose in his button-hole; under one arm he carried a silver-headed cane, and smoke curled from a big cigar that he held in his right hand. He had a heavy moustache, waxed at the ends, a saucy look in his eye, and in his bearing an arrogant swagger. In this tie was a horseshoe in diamonds. He looked like a publican dressed up in his best to go to the Derby.

'I'll tell you,' said Rosie. 'He was always such a perfect gentleman.'

1. THE PICTURE OF DORIAN GRAY by Oscar Wilde

2. CAKES AND ALE by William Somerset Maugham

3. THE GREAT GATSBY by F. Scott Fitzgerald

2

I scarcely know where to begin, though I sometimes facetiously place the cause of it all to Charley Furuseth's credit. He kept a summer cottage in Mill Valley, under the shadow of Mount Tamalpais, and never occupied it except when he loafed through the winter months and read Nietzsche and Schopenhauer to rest his brain. When summer came on, he elected to sweat out a hot and dusty existence in the city and to toil incessantly. Had it not been my custom to run up to see him every Saturday afternoon and to stop over till Monday morning, this particular January Monday morning would not have found me ***** on...

* * *

...one small woman," I said, my free hand petting her shoulder in the way all lovers know though never learn in school.

"My man," she said, looking at me for an instant with tremulous lids which fluttered down and veiled her eyes as she snuggled her head against my breast with a happy little sigh.

I look toward the *****. It was very close. A ***** was being lowered.

"One kiss, dear love," I whispered. "One kiss more before they come."

"And rescue us from ourselves," she completed, with a most adorable smile, whimsical as I had never seen it, for it was whimsical with love.

1. <u>THE SEA WOLF</u> by Jack London

2. <u>BUDDENBROOKS</u> by Thomas Mann

3. <u>OF MICE AND MEN</u> by John Steinbeck

1

The title of this work has not been chosen without the grave and solid deliberation which matters of importance demand from the prudent. Even its first, or general denomination, was the result of no common research or selection, although, according to the example of my redecessors, I had only to seize upon the most sounding and euphonic surname that English history or topography affords, and elect it at once as the title of my work, and the name of my hero. But, alas! What could my readers have expected from the chivalrous epithets of Howard, Mordaunt, Mortimer, or Stanley, or from the softer and more sentimental sounds of Belmour, Belville, Belfield and Belgrave, but pages of inanity, similar to those which I have been so christened for half a century past? I must modestly admit I am too different of my own merit to place it in...

* * *

...to their youth; and to the rising generation the tale may present some ideas of the manners of their forefathers.

Yet I heartily wish that the task of tracing the evanescent manners of his own country had employed the pen of the only man in Scotland who could have done it justice,–of him so eminently distinguished in elegant literature, and whose sketches of Colonel Caustic and Umphraville are perfectluy blended with the finer traits of national character; I should in that case have blended with the finer traits of national character; I should in that case have had more pleasure as a reader, than I shall ever feel in the pride of a successful author, should these sheets confer upon me that envied distinction. And as I have inverted the usual arrangement, placing these remarks at the end of a work to which they refer, I will venture on a second violation of form, by closing the whole with a Dedication;...

1. WAVERLY by Sir Walter Scott

2. THE MASTER OF BALLANTRAE by Robert Louis Stevenson

4. JUDE THE OBSCURE by Thomas Hardy

1

"Yes, of course, it it's fine tommorrow," said Mrs. Ransay. "But you'll have to be up with the lark," she added.

To her son these words conveyed an extraordinary joy, as if it were settled, the expedition were bound to take place, and the wonder to which settled, the expedition were bound to take place, and the wonder to which he had looked forward, for years and years it seemed, was, after a night darkness and a day's sail, within touch. Since he belonged, even at the age of six, to that great clan which cannot keep this feeling separate from that, but must let future prospects, with their joys and sorrows, cloud...

* * *

..turned to her canvas. Thee it was–her picture. Yes, with all its greens and blues, its lines running up and across, its attempt at something. It would be hung in the attics, she thought; it would be destroyed. But what did that matter? She asked herself, taking up her brush again. She looked at the steps; they were empty; she looked at her canvas; it was blurred. With a sudden intensity, as if she saw it clear for a second, she drew a line there, in the centre. It was done' it was finished. Yes, she thought, laying down her brush in extreme fatigue, I have had my vision.

1. <u>TO THE LIGHTHOUSE</u> by Virginia Woolf

2. <u>A PORTRAIT OF A LADY</u> by Henry James

3. <u>FAR FROM THE MADDING CROWD</u> by Thomas Hardy

1

In the year 1775, there stood upon the borders of Epping Forest, at a distance of about twelve miles from London–measuring from the Standard in Cornhill, or rather from the spot on or near to which the Standard used to be in days of yore–a house of public entertainment called the Maypole; which fact was demonstrated too such travellers as could neither read nor write (and at that time a vast number both of travellers and stay-at-homes were in this condition) by the emblem reared on the roadside over against the house, which, if not of those goodly proportions that Maypoles were wont to present in olden times, was a fair young ash, thirty feel in height, and straight as any arrow that ever...

* * *

...horses in the stable, upon the subject of the Kettle, so often mentioned in these pages; and before the witness who overheard him could run into the house with the intelligence, and add to it upon his solemn affirmation the statement that he had heard him laugh, the bird himself advanced with fantastic steps to the very door of the bar, and there cried 'I'm a devil, I'm a devil, 'I'm a devil!" with extraordinary rapture.

From that period although he was supposed to be much affected by the death of Mr. Willet senior), he constantly practised and improved himself in the vulgar tongue; and, as he was a mere infant for a raven when ******* was grey, he was probably gone on talking to the present time.

1. BARNABY RUDGE by Charles Dickens

2. THE BLACK ARROW by Robert Louis Stevenson

3. TOM JONES by Henry Fielding

1

It is this day three hundred and forty-eight years six months and nineteen days since the good people of Pairs were awakened by a grand peal from all the bells in the three districts of the Cite, the Universite, and the Ville. The 6th of January, 1482, was, nevertheless, a day of which history has not preserved any record. There was nothing worthy of note in the event which so early set in motion the bells and the citizens of Paris. It was neither an assault of the Picards or the Burgundians, nor a procession bearing the shrine of some saint, nor a mutiny...

* * *

...One of these skeletons, which was that of a woman, had still upon it some fragments of a dress that had once been white; and about the neck was a necklace of the seeds of adrezarach, and a little silk bag braided with green beads, which was open and empty. These things were of so little value that the hangman no doubt had not thought it worth his while to take them. The other, by which this first was closely embraced, was the skeleton of a man. It was remarked that the spine was crooked, the head depressed between the shoulders, and one leg shorter than the other. There was however no rupture of the vertebrae of the neck, and it was evident that the person to whom it belonged had not been hanged. He must have come hither and died in the place. When those who found this skeleton attempted to disengage it from that which it held in its grasp it crumbled to dust.

1. THE HUNCHBACK OF NOTRE DAME by Victor Hugo

2. THE RED AND THE BLACK by Stendhal

3. FATHER GORDIOT by Honore De Balzac

1

Wilson sat on the balcony of the Bedford Hotel with his bald kneed thrust against the ironwork. It was Sunday and the Cathedral bell clanged for matins. On the other side of Bond Street, in the windows of the High School, sat the young Negresses in dark blue gym socks engaged on the interminable task of trying to wave their wiresprung hair. Wilson stroked his very young moustache and dreamed, waiting for his gin-and-bitters.

Sitting there, facing Bond Street, he had his face turned to the sea. His pallor showed how recently he had emerged from it into the port: so did his lack of interest in the schoolgirls opposite. He was...

* * *

...harsh insistence, but she winced away from the arguments of hope.

"Oh, why, why, did he have to make such a mess of things?"

Father Rank said, "It may seem an odd thing to say–when a man's as wrong as he was–but I think, from what I saw of him, that he really loved God."

She had denied just now that she felt any bitterness, but a little more of it drained out now like tears from exhausted ducts. "He certainly loved no one else," she said.

"And you may be in the right of it there, too," Father Rank replied.

1. GREEN MANSIONS by W. H. Hudson

2. TYPEE by Herman Melville

3. THE HEART OF THE MATTER by Graham Greene

3

You don't know about me, without you have read a book by the name of *************** but that ain't no matter. That book was made by Mr. Mark *****, and he told the truth, mainly. There was things which he stretched, but mainly he told the truth. That is nothing. I never seen anybody but lied, one time or another, without it was Aunt Polly, or the widow, or maybe Mary. Aunt Polly–***** Aunt Polly, she is–and Mary, and the Widow Douglas, is all told about in that book–which is mostly a true book; with some stretchers, as I said before.

Now the way the ****** windws up, is this: ***** and me found the money that the robbers hid...

* * *

...you come in? Well, den, you k'n git yo' money when you wants it; kase dat wuz him.'

***** most well, now, and got his bullet around his neck on a watchguard for a watch, and is always seeing what time it is, and so there ain't nothing more to write about, and I am rotten glad of it, because if I'd knowed what a troule it was to make a book I wouldn't a tackled it and ain't agoing to no more. But I reckon I gotto light out for the Territory ahead of the rest, because Aunt Sally she's going to adopt me and sivilize me and I can't stand it. I been there before.

1. TOBACCO ROAD by Erskine Caldwell

2. THE SOUND AND THE FURY by William Faulkner

3. HUCKLEBERRY FINN by Mark Twain

3

I suppose that very few casual readers of the New York Herald of August 13th observed, in an obscure corner, among the "Deaths," the announcement,--

"******* on board U.S. Corvette Levant,
Lat 2° 11'S., Long. 131° W., on the
11th of May, ****"

I happened to observe it, because I was stranded at the old Mission-House in Mackinaw, waiting for a Lake Superior streamer which did not choose to come, and I was devouring to the very stubble all the current literature I could get hold of, even down to the deaths and marriages...

* * *

...even a heavenly: wherefore God is not ashamed to be called their God: for he hath prepared for them a city.'

"On this slip of paper he had written,-

"Bury me in the sea; it has been my home, and I love it. But will not some one set up stone for my memory at Fort Adams or at Orleans, that my disgrace may not be more than I ought o bear? Say on it–

"In Memory of

"*************,

"'Lieutenant in the Army of the United States.

"He loved his country as no other man has loved her; but no man deserved less at her hands."

1. THE RED BADGE OF COURAGE by Stephen Crane

2. THE MAN WITHOUT A COUNTRY by Edward Everett Hale

3. PRIDE AND PREJUDICE by Jane Austin

2

Once upon a time and very good time it was there was a moocow coming down along the road and this moocow that was coming down along the road met a nicens little boy named tuckoo...

His father told him that story: his father looked at him through a glass: he had a hairy face.

He was baby tuckoo. The moocow came down the road where Betty Byrne lived: she sold lemon platt.

O, the wild rose blossoms
On the little green place.

He sang that song. That was his song.

O, the green woth...

* * *

...with their company as they call to me, their kinsman, making ready to go, shaking the wings of their exultant and terrible youth.

26 April: Mother is putting my new secondhand clothes in order. She prays now, she says, that I may learn in my own life and away from home and friends what the heart is and what it feels. Amen. So be it. Welcome. O life! I go to encounter for the millionth time the reality of experience, and to forge in the smithy of my soul the uncreated conscience of my race.

27 April: Old father, old artificer, stand me now and ever in good stead.

1. ULYSSES by James Joyce

2. A PORTRAIT OF THE ARTIST AS A YOUNG MAN by James Joyce

3. FINNEGAN'S WIFE by James Joyce

2

Someone must traduced Joseph K., for without having done anything wrong he was arrested one fine morning. His landlady's cook, who always brought him his breakfast at eight o'clock, failed to appear on this occasion. That had never happened before. K. waited for a little while longer, watching from his pillow the old lady opposite, who seemed to be peering at him with a curiosity unusual even for her, but then, feeling both put out and hungry, he rang the bell. At once there was a knock at the door and a man entered whom he had never seen before in the house. He was slim and yet well knit, he wore a closely fitting black suit, which...

* * *

...but it cannot withstand a man who wants to go on living. Where was the Judge whom he had never seen? Where was the High Court, to which he had never penetrated? He raised his hands and spread out all his fingers.

But the hands of one of the partners were already at K.'s throat, while the other thrust the knife deep into his heart and turned it there twice. With failing eyes K. could still see the two of them immediately before him, cheek leaning against cheek, watching the final act. "Like a dog!" he said' it was as if the shame of it must outlive him.

1. STEPPENWOLF by Herman Hesse

2. THE TRIAL by Franz Kafka

3. BUDDENBROOKS by Thomas Mann

2

Lov Bensey trudged homeward through the deep white sand of the gullywashed ************* with a sack of winter turnips on his back. He had put himself to a lot of trouble to get the turnips; it was a long and tiresome walk all the way to Fuller and back gain.

The day before, Lov had heared that a man over there was selling winter turnips for fifty cents a bushel, so he had already walked seven and a half miles, and it was a mile and a half yet back to his house...

* * *

...place. The tall brick chimney standing blackened and tomb-like in the early morning sunlight was the only thing that he could see.

Dude took his hand off the horn-button and looked back at Lov.

"I reckon I'll get me a mule somewhere and some seed-cotton and guano, and grow me a crop of cotton this year," Dude said. "It feels to me like it's going to be a good year for cotton. Maybe I could grow me a bale to the acre, like Pa was always talking about doing."

1. TOBACCO ROAD by Erskine Caldwell

2. THE SOUND AND THE FURY by William Faulkner

3. OF MICE AND MEN by John Steinbeck

1

The sublimity connected with vastness is familiar to every eye. The most abstruse, the most far-reaching, perhaps the most chastened of the poet's thoughts, crowd on the imagination as he gazes into the depths of the illimitable void. The expanse of the ocean is seldom seen by the novice with indifference; and the maid, even in the obscurity of night, finds a parallel to that grandeur which seems inseparable from images that the senses cannot compass. With feelings akin to this admiration and awe–the offspring of sublimity–were the different characters with which the action of this tale must open, gazing on the scene before...

* * *

...over her still lovely face, that lasted many a day.

As for June, the double loss of husband and tribe produce the effect that ************ had foreseen. She died in the cottage of Mabel, on the shores of the lake; and Jasper conveyed her body to the island, where he interred it by the side of that of Arrowhead.

Lundie lived to marry his ancient love, and retired, a war-worn and battered veteran: but his name has been rendered illustrious in our own time, by the deeds of a younger brother, who succeeded to his territorial title, which, however, was shortly after merged in one earned by his valor on the ocean.

1. <u>DRUMS ALONG THE MOHAWK</u> by Walter Edmonds

2. <u>THE PATHFINDER</u> by James Fenimore Cooper

3. <u>THE RED BADGE OF COURAGE</u> by Stephen Crane

2

The *********** of the New York Post-Dispatch (Are you in trouble?–Do you need advice?–Write to *********** and she will help you) sat at his desk and stared at a piece of white cardboard. On it a prayer had been printed by Shrike, the feature editor.

"Soul of ******** glorify me.
Body of ******** glorify me.
Blood of ******** intoxicate me.
Tears of ******* wash me.
Oh good ******* excuse my plea.
And hide me in your heart.
And defend...

* * *

...continued his charge. He did not understand the cripple's shout and heard it as a cry for help from Desperate, Harold S. Catholic-mother, Broken-hearted, Broad-shoulders, Sick-of-it-all, Disillusioned-with-tubercular-husband. He was running to succor them with love.

The cripple turned to escape, but he was too close and ********* caught him.

While they were struggling, Betty came in through the street door. She called to them to stop and started up the stairs. The cripple saw her cutting off his escape and tried to get rid of the package. He pulled his hand out. The gun inside the package exploded and ********* fell, dragging the cripple with him. They both rolled part of the way down the stairs.

1. MISS LONELYHEARTS by Nathaniel West

2. THE SHOES OF THE FISHERMAN by Morris West

3. BABBITT by Sinclair Lewis

1

William Sylvanus Baxter paused for a moment of thought in front of the drug-store at the corner of Washington Street and Central Avenue. He had an internal question to settle before he entered the store: we wished to allow the young man at the soda-fountain no excuse for saying, "Well make up your mind what's it's goin' to be, can't you?" Rudeness of this kind, especially in the presence of girls and women, was hard to bear, and though William Sylvanus Baxter had borne it upon occasion, he had reached an age when he found it intolerable. Therefore, to avoid offering opportunity for anything of the kind, he decided upon chocolate and strawberry, mixed, before approaching the fountain...

* * *

...seeking through a veil for William's eyes. Yes, if great M. Maeterlinck is right, it seems that William ought to have caught at least some eerie echo of that wedding march, however faint–some bars or strains adrift before their time upon the moonlight of this September night in his eighteenth year.

For there, beyond the possibility of any fate to intervene, or of any later vague, fragmentary memory of even Miss Pratt to impair, there in that moonlight was his future before him.

He started forward furiously. "You-you-you little-"

But he paused, not wasting his breath upon the empty air.

His bride-to-be was gone.

1. SEVENTEEN by Booth Tarkington

2. MAIN STREET by Sinclair Lewis

3. HEAVEN'S MY DESTINATION by Thornton Wilder

1

I was ever of opinion that the honest man who married and brought up a large family did more service than he who continued single and only talked of population. From this motive, I had scarce taken ***** a year before I began to think seriously of matrimony, and chose my wife as she did her wedding gown, not for a fine glossy surface, but such qualities as would wear well. To do her justice, she was a good-natured notable woman; and as for breeding, there were few country ladies who at that time could show more. She could read any English book without...

* * *

...the two Miss Flamboroughs would have died with laughing. As soon as dinner was over, according to my old custom, I requested that the table might be taken away, to have the pleasure of seeing all my family assembled once more by a cheerful fire-side. My two little ones sat upon each knee, the rest of the company by their partners. I had nothing now on this side of the grave to wish for, all my cares were over, my pleasure was unspeakable. It now only remained that my gratitude in good fortune should exceed my former submission in adversity.

1. THE VICAR OF WAKEFIELD by Oliver Goldsmith

2. JUDE THE OBSCURE by Thomas Hardy

3. TOM JONES by Henry Fielding

1

Up to the time George Weber's father died, there was some unforgiving souls in the town of Libya Hill who spoke of him as a man who not only had deserted his wife and child, but had consummated his iniquity by going off to live with another woman. In the main, those facts are correct. As to the construction that may be placed upon them, I can only say that I should prefer to leave the final judgement to God Almighty, or to those numerous deputies of His whom He has apparently appointed as His spokesmen on this earth. In Libya Hill there are quite a number of them, and I am willing to let them do the talking. For my own part, I can only say the naked facts of John WEBer's desertion are true enough, and that none of his friends ever attempted to deny them. Aside from that, it is...

* * *

"...warm and common mucus of the earth-nasturtium smells, the thought of parlors and the good stale smell, the sudden brooding stretch of absence of the street car after it had gone, and a feeling touched with desolation hoping noon would come."

"That was your own–the turnings of the Worm" his Body said.

"And then Crane's cow again, and morning, morning in the thickets of the memory, and so many lives-and-deaths of life so long ago, together with the thought of Winter howling in the oak, so many sunlights that had come and gone since morning, morning, and all lost voices–'Son, where are you?'–of lost kinsmen in the mountains long ago...That was a good time then.

"Yes," said Body. "But–you can't go *******"

1. THE WEB AND THE ROCK by Thomas Wolfe

2. THE SOUND AND THE FURY by William Faulkner

3. APPOINTMENT IN SAMMARA by John O'Hara

1

One fine morning in the full London season, Major *********** came over from his lodgings, according to his custom, to breakfast at a certain Club in pall Mall, of which he was a chief ornament At a quarter-past ten the Major invariably made his appearance in the best blacked boots in all London, with a checked morning cravat that never was rumpled until dinner time, a buff waistcoast which bore the crown of his sovereign on the buttons, and linen so spotless that Mr. Brummel himself asked the name of his laundress, and would probably have employed her had not misfortunes compelled that great man to fly the country. ********* coat, his white gloves, his whiskers, his very cane, were perfect...

* * *

...has been so settled by the Ordainer of the lottery. We own, and see daily, how the false and worthless live and prosper, while the good are called away, and the dear and young perish untimely,–we perceive in every man's life the maimed unhappiness, the frequent falling, the bootless endeavor, the struggle of Right and Wrong, in which the strong often succumb and the swift fail; we see flowers of good blooming in foul places, as, in the most lofty and splendid fortunes, flaws of vice and meanness, and stains of evil; and, knowing how mean the best of us is, let us give a hand of charity to with all his faults and shortcomings, who does not claim to be a hero, but only a man and brother.

1. BARCHESTER TOWERS by Anthony Trollope

2. PENDENNIS by William Makepeace Thackeray

3. PRIDE AND PREJUDICE by Jane Austen

2

Six months at sea! Yes, reader, as I live, six months out of sight of land; cruising after the sperm-whale beneath the scorching sun of the Line, and tossed on the billows of the wide-rolling Pacific–the sky above, the sea around, and nothing else! Weeks and weeks ago our fresh provisions were all exhausted. There is not a sweet potato left; not a single yam. Those glorious bunches of bananas which once decorated our stern and quarter-deck have, alas, disappeared! And the delicious oranges which hung suspended from our tops and stays–they, too, are gone! Yes, they are all departed, and there is nothing left us but salt-horse and sea-biscuit. Oh! Ye...

* * *

...off his duty, has awakened the senseless clamours of those who narrow-minded suspicions blind them to a proper appreciation of measures which unusual exigencies may have rendered necessary.

It is almost needless to add that the British cabinet never had any idea of appropriating the islands; and it furnishes a sufficient vindication of the acts of Lord George Paulet, that he not only received the unqualified approbation of his own government, but that to this hour the great body of the Hawaiian people invoke blessing on his head, and look back with gratitude to the time when his literal and paternal sway diffused peace and happiness among them.

1. LORD JIM by Joseph Conrad

2. TYPEE by Herman Melville

3. TWO YEARS BEFORE THE MAST by Richard H. Dana, Jr.

2

The company stood at attention, each man looking straight ahead before him at the empty parade ground, where the cinder piles showed purple with evening. On the wind that smelt of barracks and disinfectant there was a faint greasiness of food cooking. At the other side of the wide field long lines of men shuffled slowly into the narrow wooden shanty that was the mess hall. Chins down, chests out, legs twitching and tired from the afternoon's drilling, the company stood at attention. Each man stared straight in front of him, some vacantly with resignation, some trying to amuse themselves by noting minutely every object in their field of vision,–the cinder piles, the long shadows...

* * *

...your stuff togther."

"I have nothing."

"All right, walk downstairs slowly in front of me."

Outside the windmill was turning, turning, against the piled white clouds of the sky.

Andrews turned his eyes towards the door. The M.P. closed the door after them, and followed on his heels down the steps.

On John Andrew's writing table the brisk wind rustled among the broad sheets of paper. First one sheet, then another, blew off the table, until the floor was littered with them.

1. THE NAKED AND THE DEAD by Norman Mailer

2. ALL QUIET ON THE WESTERN FRONT by Erich Maria Remarque

3. THREE SOLDIERS by John Dos Passos

3

"Turn around, my boy! How ridiculous you look! What sort of a priest's cassock have you got on! Does everybody at the academy dress like that?"

"With such words did old ******* greet his two sons, who had been absent for their education at the Royal Seminary of Kief, and had now returned home to their father.

His sons had but just dismounted from their horses. They were a couple of stout lads who still looked bashful, as became youths recently released from the seminary. Their firm healthy faces were covered with the first down of manhood, down which had...

* * *

...flames, or power be found on Earth which are capable of overpowering Russian strength?

Broad is the river Dniester, and in it are many deep pools, dense reed-beds, clear shallows and little bays; it watery mirror gleams, filled with the melodious plaint of the swan, the proud wild goose glides swiftly over it; and snipe, red-throated ruffs and other birds are to be found among the reeds and along the banks. The Cossacks rowed swiftly on in the narrow double-ruddered boats–rowed stoutly, carefully shunning the sand bars, and cleaving the ranks of the birds, which took wing–rowed, and talked of their hetman.

1. TARAS BULBA by Nickolai V. Gogol

2. THE BROTHERS KARAMAZOV by Fyodor Dostoevski

3. FATHERS AND SONS by Ivan Turgenev

1

'Kaspar! Makan!'

The well-known shrill voice startled ********* from his dream of splendid fortune into the unpleasant realities of the present hour. An unpleasant voice too. He had heard it for many years, and with every year he liked it less. No matter; there would be an end to all this soon.

He shuffled uneasily, but took no further notice of the call. Leaning with both his elbows on the balustrade of the verandah, he went on looking fixedly at the great river that flowed–indifferent and hurried–before his eyes. He liked to look at it about the time of sunset; perhaps because at that time the sinking sun would spread a glowing gold tinge...

* * *

...that makes up a life; and before him was only the end. Prayer would fill up the remainder of the days allotted to the True Believer! He took in his hand the beads that hung at his wasit.

'I found him here, like this, in the morning," said Ali, in a low and awed voice.

Abdulla glanced coldly once more at the serene face.

'Let us go,' he said, addressing Reshid.

And as they passed through the crowd that fell back before them, the beads in Abdulla's hand clicked, while in a solemn whisper he breathed out piously the name of Allah! The Merciful! The Compassionate!

1. ALMAYER'S FOLLY by Joseph Conrad

2. TARAS BULBA by Nickolai V. Gogol

3. KING SOLOMON'S MINES by H. Rider Haggard

1

Four individuals, in whose fortunes we should be glad to intersect the reader, happened to be standing in one of the saloons of the sculpture-gallery, in the Capitol, at Rome. It was that room (the first, after ascending the staircase) in the centre of which reclines the noble and most pathetic figure of the Dying Gladiator, just sinking into his death swoon. Around the walls stand the Antinous, the Amazon, the Lycian Apollo, the Juno; all famous productions of antique sculpture, and still shining in the undiminished majesty and beauty of their ideal, life although the marble, that embodies them, is yellow with time, and perhaps corroded by the damp earth in which they lay...

* * *

...former wearer. Thus, the Etruscan bracelet became the connecting bond of a series of seven wondrous tales, all of which, as they were dug out of seven sepulchres, were characterized by a sevenfold sephulchral gloom; such as Miriam's imagination, shadowed by her own misfortunes, was wont to fling over its most sportive flights.

And, now, happy as Hilda was, the bracelet brought the tears into her eyes, as being, in its entire circle, the symbol of as sad a mystery as any that Miriam had attached to the separate gems. For, what was Miriam's life to be? And where was Donatello? But Hilda had a hopeful soul, and saw sunlight on the mountain-tops.

1. THE MARBLE FAUN by Nathaniel Hawthorne

2. BEN HUR: A TALE OF THE CHRIS by Lewis (Lew) Wallace

3. QUO VADIS by Henry Sienkiewicz

1

At nine o'clock the auditorium of the Theatre des Varietes was still virtually empty; a few people were waiting in the dress circle and the stalls, lost among the red velvet armchairs, in the half-light of the dimly glowing chandelier. The great red pattch of the curtain was plunged in shadow, and not a sound came from the stage, the extinguished footlights, or the deks of the absent musicians. Only up above in the gallery, around the rotunda of the ceiling, on which naked women and children were flying about in a sky turned green by a gas, shouts and laughter emerged from a continuous din of voices, and rows of heads in caps and bonnets could be seen under the wide bays framed in...

* * *

...large reddish crust starting on one of the cheeks was invading the mouth, twisting it into a terrible grin. And around this grotesque and horrible mask of death, the hair, the beautiful hair, still blazed like sunlight and flowed in a stream of gold. Venus was decomposing. It was as if the poison she had picked up in the gutters, from the carcases left there by the roadside, that ferment with which she had poisoned a whole people, had now risen to her face and rotted it.

The room was empty. A great breath of despair came up from the boulevard and filled the curtains.

"To Berlin! To Berlin! To Berlin!"

1. NANA by Emile Zola

2. THE RED AND THE BLACK by Stendhal

3. THE TOILERS OF THE SEA by Victor Hugo

1

It had lately become common chatter at Brightwood Hospital–better known for three hundred miles around Detroit as Hudson's Clinic–that te chief was all but dead on his feet. The whole place buzzed with it.

All the way from the inquisitive solarium on the top floor to the garrulous kitchen in the basement, little groups–convalescents in wheeled chairs, nurses with tardy trays, lean internes on rubber soles, grizzled orderlies training damp mops–met to whisper and separated to disseminate the bad news. Doctor Hudson was on the verge of collapse.

On the verge?...Indeed! One lengthening...

* * *

...said softly. "I know."

Bobby's arms tightened about her.

"How did you know?" he grinned, boyishly.

"Well–let's see. You wired it to Doctor Dawson, and he wired it Marion, and she wired it to me... Awfully roundabout way to learn one was being married, wasn't it?"

"But–but–you're for it, aren't you?" he pleaded, searching her eyes.

She smiled.

"Perhaps we should go abroad, bobby. We're blocking the traffic."

1. BABBIT by Sinclair Lewis

2. HEAVEN'S MY DESTINATION by Thornton Wilder

3. MAGNIFICENT OBSESSION by Lloyd C. Douglas

3

You have requested me, my dear friend, to bestow some of that leisure with which Providence has blessed the decline of my life in registering the hazards and difficulties which attended its commencement. The recollection of those adventures, as you are pleased to term them, has indeed left upon my mind a checkered and varied feeling of pleasure and pain, mingled, I trust, with no slight gratitude and veneration to the Disposer of human events, who guided my early course through much risk and labor, that the ease, with which he has blessed my prolonged life might seem softer from remembrance and contrast. Neither is it possible for me to doubt, what you have often affirmed, that the incidents which befell me among a people singularly primitive...

* * *

...as much regularity as the proprietors did their ordinary rents. It seemed impossible that his life should have concluded without a violent end. Nevertheless, he died in old age and by a peaceful death, some time about the year 1733, and is still remembered in his country as the Robin Hood of Scotland, the dread of the wealthy, but the friend of the poor, and possessed of many qualities, both of head and heart, which would have graced a less equivocal profession than that to which fate condemned him.

Old Andrew Fairservice used to say that "There were many thing ower bad for blessing, and ower gude for banning, like *******."

1. KIDNAPPED by Robert Louis Stevenson

2. ROB ROY by Sir Walter Scott

3. THE THREE MUSKETEERS by Alexander Dumas, Sr.

2

Nobody could sleep. When morning came, assault craft would be lowered and a first wave of troops would ride through the surf and charge ashore on the beach at Anopepei. All over the ship, all through the convey, there was a knowledge that in a few hours some of them were going to be dead.

A soldier lies flat on his bunk, closes his eyes, and remains wide-awake. All about him, like the soughing of surf, he hears the murmurs of men dozing fitfully. "I won't do it, I won't do it," someone cries out of a dream, and the soldier opens his eyes and gazes slowly about the hold, his vision becoming lost in the intricate tangle of hammocks and naked bodies and dangling equipment. He decides he want to go to the head, and cursing...

* * *

...was goddamned if he's make a fool of himself filling out a requisition for that. Maybe Chaplain Davis, who was a good egg–but no, he'd better not ask him.

Dalleson scratched his head. He could write a letter to Army Headquarters, Special Services. They probably wouldn't have Grable, but any pin-up girl would do.

That was it. He'd write Army. And in the meantime he might send a letter to the War Departments Training Aids Section. They were out for improvements like that. The Major could see every unit in the Army using his idea at last. He clenched his fists with excitement.

Hot dog!

1. LORD JIM by Joseph Conrad

2. A BELL FOR ADANO by John Hersey

3. THE NAKED AND THE DEAD by Norman Mailer

3

In that pleasant district of merry England which is watered by the river Don, there extended in ancient times a large forest, covering the greater part of the beautiful hills and valleys which lie between Sheffield and the pleasant town of Doncaster. The remains of this extensive wood are still to be seen at the noble seats of Wentworth, of Wharncliffe Park, and around Rotherham. Here haunted of yore the fabulous Dragon of Wantley; here were fought many of the most desperate battles during the Civil Wars of the Roses; and here also flourished in ancient times those bands of gallant outlaws whose deeds have been rendered so popular in English song.

Such being our chief scene, the date...

* * *

...higher but for the premature death of the heroic Coeur-de-Lion, before the Castle of Chaluz, near Lamoges. With the life of a generous, but rash and romantic, monarch perished all the projects which his ambition and his generosity had formed; to whom may be applied, with a slight alteration, the lines composed by Johnson for Charles of Sweden–

His fate was destined to a foreign strand
A petty fortress and an 'humble' hand;
He left the name at which the world grew pale,
To point of a moral, or adorn a TALE.

1. A CONNECTICUT YANKEE IN KING ARTHUR'S COURT by Mark Twain

2. IVANHOE by Sir Walter Scott

3. THE BLACK ARROW by Robert Louis Stevenson

2

A destiny that leads the English to the Dutch is strange enough; but one that leads from the Epsom into Pennsylvania, and thence into the hills that shut in Alamont over the proud coral cry of the cock, and the soft stone smile of an angel, is touched by that dark miracle of change which makes new magic in a dusty world.

Each of us is all the sums he has not counted: subtract us into nakedness and night again, and you shall see begin in Crete four thousand years ago the love that ended yesterday in Texas.

The seed of our destruction will blossom in the desert, the alexin of our cure grows by a mountain rock, and our lives are haunted by a Georgian slattern, because a London cutpurse went unhung. Each moment is the fruit of forty thousand years. The minute-winning...

* * *

...came, and the song of waking birds, and the Square, bathed in the young pearl light of morning. And a wind stirred lightly in the Square, and, as he looked, Ben, like a fume of smoke, was melted into dawn.

And the angels on Gant's porch were frozen in hard marble silence, and at a distance life awoke, and there was a rattle of lean wheels, a slow clangor of shod hoofs. As he heard the whistle wail along the river.

Yet, as he stood for the last time by the angels of his father's porch, it seemed as if the Square already were far and lost; or, I should say, he was like a man who stands upon a hill above the town he has left, yet does not say "The town is near," but turns his eyes upon the distant soaring ranges.

1. AN AMERICAN TRAGEDY by Theodore Dreiser

2. APPOINTMENT AT SAMMARA by John O'Hara

3. LOOK HOMEWARD, ANGEL by Thomas Wolfe

3

I have returned, finally, from my two week's absence. My friends have been here, in Roulettenberg, for three days already. I thought that they would be expecting me God knows how eagerly, but I was wrong. The General had an extremely uncorned air, talked to me condescendingly for a few minutes, then sent me off to his sister. Clearly, they had managed to borrow some money along the way. It even appeared to me that the General looked somewhat embarrassed. Maria Filippovna seemed to be extremely busy and barely exchanged a few words with me. She took the momey, however, counted...

* * *

...its rich sparkle, giving everything a joyous appearance. Everybody was busy with their daily activities. People were working, buying, selling, and talking, talking especially about the young woman whose body had been found in the river a short time earlier. It was assumed that she had fallen into the water as she was crossing the river using a narrow footbridge, since the body was found not far from the bridge, and in the very middle of the stream, where it flowed faster. She must have become dizzy when looking into the rapidly flowing waters, though the Lord, who sees the intentions as well as the deeds of men, knows better. But we, on our part, shall neither reject nor affirm such supposition.

1. THE GAMBLER by Fyodor Dostoevski

2. FATHERS AND SONS by Ivan Turgenev

3. DEAD SOULS by Nikolai V. Gogol

1

During the early part of the month of March, in the year 1841, I traveled in *********.

There is nothing more agreeable than a journey through this picturesque country. Embarking on Toulon, you arrive in twenty hours at Ajaccio, or in twenty-four hours at Bastia, where you can hire a horse for five francs per day; or purchase one for a hundred and fifty francs. Do not smile at the poorness of this price; the animal which you thus hire or buy, like that famous horse of the Gascon, which jumped from the Pont-Neuf into the Seine, does things which neither Prospero nor Nautilus could do, those heroes of the races of...

* * *

...a sigh, or made a movement. I went up to him, impelled by that invincible curiosity which urges us to follow a catastrophe to the end. The bullet had entered the temple, at the very spot predicted by Lucien the day before.

I ran up to him; he had remained calm and motionless. But upon seeing me within his reach, he dropped his pistol and threw himself into my arms.

"Oh! My *****! My poor *****!" exclaimed he.

He broke out into sobs!

These were the first tears the young man had ever shed!

1. THE MARBLE FAUN by Nathaniel Hawthorne

2. THE CORSICAN BROTHERS by Alexander Dumas, Sr.

3. LES MISERABLES by Victor Hugo

2

********* jaw was long and bony, his chin a jutting v under the more flexible v of his mouth. His nostrils curved back to make another smaller, v. His yellow-grey eyes were horizontal. The v-motif was picked up again by thickish brows rising outward from twin creases above a hooked nose, and his pale brown hair grew down–from high flat temples–in a point on his forehead. He looked rather pleasantly like a blond Satan. He said to Effire Perine: "Yes, sweetheart?"

She was a lanky sunburned girl whose tan dress of thin woolen stuff clung to her with an effect of dampness. Her eyes were brown and playful...

* * *

...that." He snapped his fingers.
She escaped from his arm as if it had hurt her. "Don't, please, don't touch me," she said brokenly. "I know–I know you're right. You're right. But don't touch me now–not now." ********* face became pale as his collar. The corridor-door's knob rattled. Effie Perrine turned quickly and went into the outer office, shuttting the door behind her. When she came in again she shut it behind her. She said in a small flat voice: "Iva is here."

********* looking at his desk, nodded almost imperceptibly. "Yes," he said, and shivered. "Well, send her in."

1. <u>CASS TIMBERLANE</u> by Sinclair Lewis

2. <u>THE MALTESE FAlCON</u> by Dashiell Hammett

3. <u>ELMER GANTRY</u> by Sinclair Lewis

2

My father, ********* of Santillane, after having borne arms for a long time in the Spanish service, retired to his native place. There he married a chamber-maid who was not exactly in her teens, and I made my debut on this stage ten months after marriage. They aftwerwards went to live at Oviedo, where my mother got into service, and my father obtained a situation equally adapted to his capacities as a squire. As their wages were their fortune, I might have got my education as I could, had it not been for an uncle of mine in the town, a canon, by name *********. He was my mother's eldest brother, and my godfather. Figure to yourself a little fellow, three feet and a half high, as fat as you can conceive, with a head...

* * *

...he did not repay it with ingratitude. In short, we were a happy and united family: we could scarcely bear the interval of separation between evening and morning. Our time was divided between Lirias and Jutella: his excellency's pistoles made the old battlements to raise their heads afgain, and the castle to resume its lordly port.

For these three years, reader, I have led a life of unmixed bliss in this beloved society. To perfect my satisfaction, heaven has designed to send me two smiling babes, whose education will be the amusement of my declining years; and if every husband might venture to hazard so bold an hypothesis, I devoutly believe myself their father.

1. GIL BLAS by Alain Rene Le Sage

2. THE RED AND THE BLACK by Stendhal

3. THE TOILERS OF THE SEA by Victor Hugo

1

I. Ferryslip

Three gulls wheel above the broken boxes,
orangerinds, spoiled cabbage heads that heave
between the splintered plank walls, the green waves
spume under the round bow as the ferry, skidding on
the tide, crashes, gulps, the broken water, slides,
settles slowly into the slip. Handwicnches whirl
with jungle of chains. Gates fold upwards, feet
out across the crack, men and women press through
the manuresmelling wooden tunnel of the ferryhouse,
crushed and jostling like apples fed down a chute
into a press

The nurse, holding the basket at arm's...

* * *

...walks fast to get out of the smell. He is hungry; his shoes are beginning to raise blisters on his big toes. At a cross-road where the warning light still winks and winks, is a gasoline station, opposite it the Lightning Bug lunchwagon. Carefully he spends his last quarter on breakfast. That leaves him three cents for good luck, or bad for that matter. A huge furniture truck, shiny and yellow, has drawn up outside.

"Say will you give me a lift?" he asks the redhaired man at the wheel.

"How fur ye goin?"

"I dunno.... Pretty far."

1. MANHATTAN TRANSFER by John Dos Passos

2. TWO YEARS BEFORE THE MAST by Richard Henry Dana Jr.

3. LORD JIM by Joseph Conrad

1

About fifteen years ago, at the end of the second decade of this century, four people were standing together on the platform of the railway station of a town in the hills of western Catawba. This little station, really just a suburban adjunct of the larger town which, behind the concealing barrier of a rising ground, sept away a mile or two to the west and north, had become in recent years the popular point of arrival and departure for travellers to and from the cities of the east, and now, in fact, accommodated a much larger traffic than did the central station of the town, which was situated two miles westward around the powerful bend of the rails. For this reason a considerable number of people were now assembled here, and from their words and gestures, a quietly suppressed excitement that somehow seemed...

***

...centre and the target of his life, the image of immortal one-ness that again collected him to one, and hurled the whole collected passion, power and might of his one life into the blazing certitude, the immortal goverance and unity, of love.

"Set me a seal upon thine heart, as a seal upon thine arm: for love is strong as death' jealousy is cruel as the grave: the coals thereof are coals of fire, which hath a most vehement flame."

And now all the faces pass in through the ship's great side (the tender flower face among them). Proud, potent faces of rich Jews, alive with wealth and luxury, glow in rich, lighted cabins; the doors are closed, and the ship is given to the darkness and the sea.

1. <u>OF TIME AND THE RIVER</u> by Thomas Wolfe

2. <u>LIE DOWN IN DARKNESS</u> by William Styron

3. <u>SHIP OF FOOLS</u> by Katherine Anne Porter

1

All true histories contain instruction; though, in some, the treasure may be hard to find, and, when found, so trivial in quantity, that the dry, shrivelled kernel scarefly compensates for the trouble of cracking the nut. Whether this be the case with my history or not, I am hardly competent to judge. I sometimes think it might prove useful to some, and entertaining to others; but the world may judge for itself. Shielded by my own obscurity, and by the lapse of years, and a few fictitious names, I do not fear to venture; and will candidly lay before the public what I would not disclose to the most intimate friend.

My father was a clergyman of the north...

* * *

..is entirely without), I defy anybody to blame him as a pastor, a husband, or a father.

Our children, Edward, *****, and little Mary, promise well; their education, for the time being, is chiefly committed to me; and they shall want no good thing that a mother's care can give. Our modest income is amply sufficient for our requirements: and by practising the economy we learnt in harder times, and never attempting to imitate our richer neighbours, we manage not only to enjoy comfort and contentment ourselves, but to have every year something to lay by for our children, and something to give to those who need it.

And now I think I have said sufficient.

1. AGNES GREY by Anne Bronte

2. MOLL FLANDERS by Daniel Defoe

3. BARCHESTER TOWERS by Anthony Trollope

1

"The barometer of his emotional nature was set for a spell of riot."

These words, on the printed page, had the unsettling effect no doubt intended, but with a difference. At once he put the book aside: closed it, with his fingers still between the pages; dropped his arm over the edge of the chair and let it hang, the book somewhere near the floor. This in case he wanted to look at it again. But he did not need to. Already he knew the sentence by heart: he might have written it to himself. Indeed, it was with a sense of familiarity, of recognition, that his mind had first read through and accepted that sentence only a moment before; and now, as he relaxed his fingers' grip and dropped the book...

* * *

...little tower. He admired his steady hand, his untrembling hand, as he arranged the half-dollars on the bottom, then quarters next, then nickels, then pennies, with the dimes on top. That would satisfy Wick. Satisfy anybody.

He hurried back to his room. He poured another drink, drank it, and crawled in, feeling like a million dollars.

He lay listening now for Wick. Let him come any time now. The thing was over. He himself was back home in bed again and safe. God knows why or how but had to come through one more. Not telling what might happen the next time but why worry about that? This one was over and nothing had happened at all. Why did they make such a fuss?

1. THE LOST WEEKEND by Charles Jackson

2. BABBIT by Sinclair Lewis

3. HEAVEN'S MY DESTINATON by Thornton Wilder

1

The Atlantic wears away our coasts. The pressure of the Arctic current deforms our western cliffs. The wall which runs parallel to the coast is undermined from Saint-Valery-sur-Somme to Ingouville; large blocks of stone cumble, the water rolls clouds of pebbles, our ports are filled with sand or stones, and the mouths of our rivers are barred. Every day a portion of Norman earth is detached and disappears under the waves. This prodigious work, now abated, has been terrible. The immence buttress of Finistere was a necessity to keep the sea back. One may judge of the strength of the flow of the Arctic current, and of the violence of its effects, by the hollow which it has made between Cherbourg...

***

...eyes, at the same time as the infinite water around he rock of Hild-Holm-'Ur.

The Cashmere, which had become invisible, was not a speck mignled with the mist. One needed to know where it was in order to be able to distinguish it.

Little by little this speck, which was no longer a form, grew pale.

Then it dwindled.

Then it disappeared.

At the moment when the vessel vanished on the horizon, the head disappeared under water. There was nothing left but the sea.

1. THE TOILERS OF THE SEA by Victor Hugo

2. CAPTAINS COURAGEOUS by Rudyard Kipling

3. TWO YEARS BEFORE THE MAST by Richard Henry Dana Jr.

1

The Loggia de' Cerchi stood in the heart of old Florence, within a labyrinth of narrow streets behind the Badia, now rarely threaded by the stranger, unless in a dubious search for a certain severely simple door-place, bearing this inscription:

AU NACQUE IL DIVINO POETA.

To the ear of Dante, the same streets rang with the shout and clash of fierce battle between rival families; but in the fifteenth century, they were only noisy with the unhistorical quarrels and broad jests of wool-carders in the clot-producing quarters of San Martino and Garbo.

Under the loggia, in the early morning of the 9th of April, 1492, two men had their eyes fixed...

* * *

...our old Piero di Cosimo and Nello coming up the Borgo Pinti, bringing us their flowers. Let us go and wave our hands to them, that they may know we see them."

"How queer old Piero is," said Lillo, as they stood at the corner of the loggia, watching the advancing figures. "He abuses you for dressing the altar, and thinking so much of Fra Girolamo, and yet be brings you the flowers."

"Never mind," said *******. "There are many good people who did not love Fra Girolamo. Perhaps I should never have learned to love him if he had not helped me when I was in great need."

1. ROMOLA by George Eliot

2. THE CHARTERHOUSE OF PARMA by Stendhal

3. THE MARBLE FAUN by Nathaniel Hawthorne

1

The British are frequently criticized by other nations for their dislike of change, and indeed we love England for those aspects of nature and life which change the least. Here in the West Country, where I was born, men are slow of speech, tenacious of opinion–and averse–beyond their countrymen elsewhere–to innovation of any sort. The houses of my neighbours, the tenants' cottages, the very fishing boats which ply on the Bristol Channel, all conform to the patterns of a simpler age. And an old man, forty of whose three-and-seventy years have been spent afloat, may be pardoned a not unnatural tenderness toward the scenes of his youth, and a satisfaction that these scenes remain so little altered...

* * *

...of my own mother, as well. "The English captain from Matavai," Tuahu was saying, and she gave me her hand graciously. My granddaughter was staring up at me in wonder, and I turned away blindly.

"We must go on," said Tehani to her uncle. "I promised the child she should see the English boat."

"Aye, go," replied Tuahu.

The moon was bright overhead when I reembarked in the pinnace to return to my ship. A chill night breeze came whispering down from the depths of the valley, and suddenly the place was full of ghosts,–shadows of men alive and dead,–my own among them.

1. CAPTAIN HORATIO HORNBLOWER by C. S. Forester

2. MUTINY ON THE BOUNTY by Charles Nordhoff & James Norman Hall

3. CAPTAINS COURAGEOUS by Rudyard Kipling

2

"You won't be late?" There was anxiety in Marjorie Carling's voice, there was something like entreaty.

"No, I won't be late," said Walter, unhappily and guiltily certain that he would be. Her voice annoyed him. It drawled a little, it was to refined–even in misery.

"Not later than midnight." She might have reminded him of the time when he never went out in the evenings without her. She might have done so; but she wouldn't; it was against her principles; she didn't want to force his love in anyway.

"Well, call it one. You know what these parties are." But as matter of fact, she didn't know, for the good reason that, not being his wife, she wasn't invited to them.

***

...so far as he was concerned. It was the end of her also as far as everybody was concerned. For some few days later, having written him a twelve-page letter, which he put in the fire after reading the first scarifying sentence, she lay down with her head in an oven and turned on the gas. But that was something which Burla could not foresee. His mood as he walked whistling homeward was one of unmixed contentment. That night he and Beatrice pretended to be two little children and had their bath together. Two little children sitting opposite ends of the big old-fashioned bath. And what a romp they had! The bathroom was drenched with their splashings. Of such is the Kingdom of Heaven.

1. POINT COUNTERPOINT by Aldous Huxley

2. OF HUMAN BONDAGE by William Somerset Maugham

3. ROOM AT THE TOP by John Braine

1

Sir Daniel and his men lay in and about Kettley that night, warmly quartered and well patrolled. But the Knight of Tunstall was one who never rested from money-getting; and even now, when was on the brink of an adventure which should make or mar him, he was up an hour after midnight to squeeze poor neighbours. He was one who trafficked greatly in disputed inheritances; it was his way to buy out the most unlikely claimant, and then, by the favour he curried with great lords about the king, procure unjust decisions in his favour; or, if that was too roundabout, to seize the disputed manor by force of arms, and rely on his influence and Sir Oliver's...

***

...affection, in each other's eyes.

Thenceforth the dust and blood of that unruly epoch passed them by. They dwelt apart from alarms in the green forest where their love began.

Two old men in the meanwhile enjoyed pensions in great prosperity and peace, and with perhaps a superfluity of ale and wine, in Tunstall hamlet. One had been all his life a shipman, and continued to the last to lament his man Tom. The other, who had been a bit of everything, turned in the end towards piety, and made a most religious death under the name of Brother Honestus in the neighbouring abbey. So Lawless had his will, and died a friar.

1. THE BLACK ARROW by Robert Louis Stevenson

2. IVANHOE by Sir Walter Scott

3. A CONNECTICUT YANKEE IN KING ARTHUR'S COURT by Mark Twain

1

It is a curious thing that at my age-I shall never see sixty again–I should find myself taking up a pen to try to write a history. I wonder what sort of a history it will be when I have finished with it, if ever I come to the end of the trip! I have done a good many things in my life, which seems a long one to me, owing to my having begun work so young perhaps. At an age when other boys are at school I was earning my living in the old Colony at natal. I have been trading, hunting, fighting or exploring ever since. And yet it is only eight months ago that I made my pile. It is a big pile now that I have got it–I don't yet know how big–but I do not think I would go through the last fifteen or sixteen months again for it; no, not if I knew...

***

...of the great bull that killed poor Khiva have now been put up in the hall here, over the pair of buffalo horns you gave me, and look magnificent; and the axe with which I chopped off Twala's head is fixed above my writing-table. I wish that we could have managed to bring away the coats of chain armour. Don't lose poor Foulata's basket in which you carried off the diamonds.

H.C.

Today is Tuesday. There is a steamer going on Friday, and I really think that I must take Curtis at his word, and sail by her for England, if only to see you, Harry, my boy, and to look after the printing of this history, which is a task that I do not like to trust anybody else.

1. KING SOLOMON'S MINES by H. Rider Haggard

2. GOODBYE, MR. CHIPS by James Hilton

3. A PASSAGE TO INDIA by E. M. Forster

1

Until Jinny Marshland was called to the stand, the Judge was deplorably sleepy.

The case of Miss Tilda Hatter vs. the City of Grand Republic had been yawning its way through testimony about a not very interesting sidewalk. Plaintiff's attorney desired to show that the city had been remarkably negligent in leaving upon that sidewalk a certain lump of ice which, on February 7, 1941, at or about the hour of 9:37 P.M., had caused the plaintiff to slip, to slide, and to be prone upon the public way, in a state of ignominy and sore pain. There had been an extravagant amount of data as to whether the lump of ice had been lurking sixteen, eighteen, or more than eighteen feet from the...

* * *

...against the light from the hall.

"I thought maybe you could come in and see me. I was very cold," she said plaintively. "Couldn't I crawl in your bed and get warm?"

Then, for her and his love for her, he gave up his vested right to be tragic, gave up pride and triumph and all the luxury of submerged resentment, and smiled at her with the simplicity of a baby.

"Dear Jinny!" he said, and she confided, "I'm going to get new storm-windows on my room, even if I have to put them up myself. I could, too! I'm the best storm-window fixer in this town. You'll see!"

1. CASS TIMBERLANE by Sinclair Lewis

2. BLEAK HOUSE by Charles Dickens

3. HEAVEN'S MY DESTINATION by Thornton Wilder

1

Riding down to Port Warwick from Richmond, the train begins to pick up speed on the outskirts of the city, past the tobacco factories with their ever-present haze of acrid, sweetish dust and past the rows of uniformly brown clapboard houses which stretch down the hilly streets for miles, the hundreds of rooftops all reflecting the pale light of dawn; past the suburban roads still sluggish and sleepy with early morning traffic, and rattling swiftly now over the bridge which separates the last two hills where in the valley below you can see the James River winding beneath its acid-green crust of scum out beside the chemical plants and more rows of clapboard houses and into the...

* * *

...Yeah! Yeah!" The train roared, trembled, came nearer. It was a ferocious noise. Stonewall stuck his fingers in his ears; the others turned their faces toward the sea. "Yes, Jesus! Yeah! Yeah!" The voice was almost drowned out. The train came on with a clatter, shaking the trestle, and its whistle went off full-blast in a spreading plume of steam. "Yeah! Yeah!" Another blast from the whistle, a roar, a gigantic sound' and it seemed to soar into the dusk beyond and above them forever, with a noise, perhaps, like the clatter of the opening of everlasting gates and doors–passed swiftly on–toward Richmond, the North, the oncoming night.

1. LIE DOWN IN DARKNESS by William Styron

2. THE SOUND AND THE FURY by William Faulkner

3. TOBACCO ROAD by Erskine Caldwell

Index of Titles

S

T

U

Made in the USA
Coppell, TX
11 July 2020